# The Body
# in the
# Record Room

## A MYSTERY

## JOE BARONE

Thomas Dunne Books
St. Martin's Minotaur ♒ New York

This is a work of fiction. All of the characters, organizations, and events portrayed in this novel are either products of the author's imagination or are used fictitiously.

THOMAS DUNNE BOOKS.
An imprint of St. Martin's Press.

THE BODY IN THE RECORD ROOM. Copyright © 2008 by Joe Barone. All rights reserved. Printed in the United States of America. St. Martin's Press, 175 Fifth Avenue, New York, N.Y. 10010.

www.minotaurbooks.com
www.thomasdunnebooks.com

Library of Congress Cataloging-in-Publication Data)

Barone, Joe, 1942–
  The body in the record room / Joe Barone.—1st St. Martin's Minotaur ed.
    p. cm.
  ISBN-13: 978-0-312-38410-4
  ISBN:10: 0-312-38410-6
  1. Mental patients—Fiction.   2. Murder—Investigation—Fiction.   3. Psychiatric hospitals—Fiction.   4. Rogers, Roy, 1911–1998—Influence—Fiction.
  5. Missouri—Fiction.   I. Title.
  PS3602.A777415B63  2008
  813'.6—dc22

                                                            2008023580

First Edition: October 2008

10   9   8   7   6   5   4   3   2   1

*Fondly dedicated to the memories of Lefty, Guy, Erliss, Rose,
Walter, Dolly, Don, and all the others with whom I grew up.
You changed my view of God and of the universe.*


*Also in memory of and with thanks to
Larry Ferguson.
He was the best writer I ever knew personally.
He taught me the craft of writing,
and in so doing, he changed my life.*

## AUTHOR'S NOTE

This novel is set in a state mental hospital in the 1950s. That institution is similar to, but not the same as, the one where I grew up. There were thousands of them across the United States in the 1950s. All the events and people in the story come from my imagination and are not real.

# ACKNOWLEDGMENTS

I have to get in line to thank Ruth Cavin. She has encouraged so many writers. She looks for ways to find new writers in a super-competitive business. Thanks, Ruth!

Also, thanks to Toni Plummer. She was always willing to answer what must have seemed to her to be the silliest of questions.

Book publishing is much more of a cooperative effort than I would have guessed. Thanks to copy editor Barbara Wild. I learned a lot from her. The errors in this book are mine, of course, but Barbara saved me from a couple of doozies. Thanks, Barbara.

And finally, thanks to Ellen Rininger, the contest reader who identified this book and sent it on to Ruth and Toni. Ellen, without you, the reader who has this book in hand right now would not have been introduced to my Roy Rogers or reminded of the real Roy Rogers and Dale Evans, two people whose positive Christian example touched so many lives.

One final comment: St. Martin's Minotaur and the writers'/readers' groups they work with have set up their contests in hopes of finding writers who might otherwise be missed. Not just as a writer, but as a reader, I thank all of you for that.

# Editor's Note

When my unmarried, childless great-uncle passed away at the age of ninety-four in 1996, I found this manuscript among his belongings. It was written in his strong, looping, spidery handwriting. For a long time, I struggled with what I should do with it. Now, for what it's worth, here it is.

# 1

## The Large Auditorium

Early that evening, I found the body in the record room, but I left it there until after the movie.

At the movie, *The Carson City Kid,* I could see myself riding across the prairie on my huge Palomino horse. I knew I was after the letter, but it involved having to chase down the stagecoach.

I knew I would catch the stagecoach, and I knew they would think I was a thief.

It was an old movie now, made back in 1940. I had Trigger, but he didn't play much of a part in the whole thing. He got stolen from me, and I had to steal him back.

As I watched the chase, the flickering black-and-white images brought it all back to me. People say I am crazy, that I'm not really Roy Rogers at all, but I know who I am.

After the movie, they released us to the wards, those of us who didn't require supervision.

The Sunrise lunatic asylum was an old Kirkbride building

with two several-storied wings, one off of each side of a large cupolaed main administration unit. They took us back, the men to the left wing and the women to the right wing, up and down the metal stairs.

I still remember the stairs. They were black metal lattice-work. You could look down through them and see the people below. We were all fairly trustworthy most of the time. The really dangerous people were in other, separate, buildings.

It was no problem to talk with Harry, to arrange to meet him after lights-out.

Harry was a young man in his early twenties with a receding hairline. He was my strong helper. After all, I was over fifty then.

# 2

## The Record Room

We're going to the record room," I told Harry quietly when I met him later. We'd be doing most of our work after midnight.

We retraced our steps back down the stairs, very quietly. At each landing, we had to be careful because of "supervision rooms," the places where the staff sometimes hung out. Harry and I had become skilled at listening and waiting and then slipping by those rooms.

Finally, we got to the darkened auditorium. Then we went through the double doors at the center back of the auditorium, into the entryway, and then into the dimly lighted corridor. Most of the building, especially the halls and entryways, was kept dimly lighted at night.

It was easy after that. You walked down the corridor a little ways, turned right, walked down another corridor, and you were in the main section of the second floor. That had the little man's office in it, as well as the business manager's office and a lot of other things.

From there, you made your way down the winding stairs, into the marbled main lobby of the building, and then back toward the record room.

The lobby was usually empty late at night. You could turn right from the foot of the stairs, walk past the Double Cola machine under the stairs—I loved Double Cola—back past the canteen on the left, and to the record room door.

God blessed me in a lot of ways. One way is that I can get into almost any locked room.

I was in the record room a lot at night. I was reading the history and plotting the asylum cemetery. The cemetery was way out on the edge of the asylum's more than one thousand acres.

They needed all those acres. After all, they had a complete farm that supplied food to feed twenty-two hundred patients and more than eight hundred employees. There were bakeries and canneries and a milk-pasteurizing plant. They had their own power plant, along with laundries and electrical shops and a whole lot else. And clear out at the edge of the place was the cemetery where they buried the abandoned patients who had died in the asylum.

Those graves were marked with numbered metal markers. There were no names, just numbers. In the record room, there was a plat map with the names and numbers keyed together. I spent my time looking in the rows and rows of filing cabinets at the records, working to put stories with those names. There were so many, I couldn't keep them all right there in my mind. I kept a little book with people's names and numbers and stories. Just because you're crazy doesn't mean you shouldn't have a name and story.

At night, the record room was a perfect place to be. Once the door was closed and locked, you could see pretty well by turning on a small lamp on a desk way back in the corner. If you were lucky, no one would even know that you were there.

• • •

I found the old man in the priest suit just before I went up to the movie. I went to the record room, and there he was. He was just lying there dead, like we all will be someday. He had been beaten and kicked, his nose broken. It looked like someone had stepped on it.

"I wonder who opened up the record room?" I said the words almost to myself, but Harry heard me.

"What?"

"This man's a stranger, Harry. He's not someone who lives or works here. I wonder who let him in?"

"Maybe it was the little man." The little man was the super-intendent of the place.

"The little man guards the record room with his life. He says it contains confidential information. He wouldn't let a stranger in."

"Well, then . . ." Harry paused. He was having trouble naming anybody else.

"We need to move him," I told Harry.

"Where?" Harry was a simple man who loved animals. He was very young back then. He had a smooth face, deep gray eyes, and coal black hair.

"Over with the horses," I said.

"Over with the horses?"

"Over with the horses. Pat and Mike. We can bury him there, and nobody will ever find him."

"In the horse barn?" Harry said, finally getting the point. "But what about his family? Won't they miss him?" I thought Harry was going to break down and cry.

"Probably not, and besides, if we tell anybody about this, there'll be all kinds of problems."

"But won't his family miss him?" Harry said.

"Even if they do, they won't know where to find him, Harry. He's not someone I've seen around here."

"Oh."

"I need to find out what's happening before we tell anyone about him."

Harry didn't answer now, but he still looked sad.

"Let's go get the horses," I said to take Harry's mind off of his preoccupation with the man's family.

It was cool in the record room. The man was still pliable. No telling how long it would be, but the time was coming soon when he'd get stiff and hard to handle. The blood had already settled into purple splotches at the bottom of his arms and, probably, other places.

Harry and I were good at putting harness on the horses. We did it a lot. The horses were useful tools if you had items to move, and sometimes we had items to move.

Pat and then Mike, the two huge sorrel draft horses with the matching white patches on their foreheads, knew us and were gentle with us.

We hooked them up to the green garbage wagon.

The hospital didn't use the horses to do the farming anymore. They had tractors. But they kept the horses and the mules to pull the garbage wagons and do things like that.

Really, it had to do with the man who ran the farm. He loved horses. He had grown up with horses. These horses were his friends. He wasn't going to take them to the sale barn or the dog food factory. He was going to keep them until they died a natural death. So the hospital—that's what they called it now; they used to call it an asylum—kept the horses.

The man in the priest suit was already beginning to get stiff by the time we laid him in the steep-sided green wagon. I crossed his arms over his chest before the stiffness set in full-time, but they kept wanting to flop back. We were going to have to stuff him in the grave.

We moved quietly. You have to do that. You can do these kinds of things at night, once in a while, but you have to be as quiet as possible.

We had carried the man out of the record room, through the employees' cafeteria, through the back hallways into the bakery with its bread smell, and then out the back door into the wagon. We took the long way around because that way had fewer street-lights. There were lights between the loading dock at the back door and the place where we turned left by the little pond. From there on, it was fairly dark.

Harry drove the wagon. He could almost talk to Pat and Mike and get them to do what he wanted.

When we got there, we backed the wagon into the barn, dug the grave, a full six feet deep. Harry was good at that. Before we buried the man, I frisked him. That's when I found the note in his pocket. That's the only thing he had, a handwritten note. Then we stuffed the man in the grave.

The grave was in Pat's stall. I figured that way, we could dig the grave, put the man in, fill the grave with dirt, cover the grave with straw, and then put Pat back in the stall. What better place to hide a body?

They changed the straw once in a while, but since Harry was the one who cleaned the stalls, we were safe. Harry loved work-ing in the horse barn.

We could both come back at night once a week or so and fill in whatever depression would occur. If we were lucky, no one would ever know the priest-suited man was there.

So that's what we did.

"Pat will poop on him," Harry said.

"Nah. Pat will poop on the ground above him," I assured Harry. By the time we had the wagon back in place and the horses back in their stalls, it was just a couple hours until daylight.

"We need to get back to the ward," I said.

Harry and I did a lot of things together, and we always seemed to get away with them, at least so far.

## A Personal Note

*Before I go any further, there are some things I have to talk about that you might not understand. They aren't dreams. They aren't even the kinds of nightmares that wake you and keep you up all night. They are real. They are huge men coming out from under the bed to come and get you. They are voices that tell you they intend to rape and kill you and no matter what you do, there's nothing you can do to stop them.*

*They come at various times and in different ways. The little man used to tell me they came when I didn't take my medicine, but back then my medicine put me down. It made my thinking lag. It tackled me in a different way, causing me to collapse and be unable to do much of anything.*

*There wasn't much effective medicine back then. Now I can write this book. I can tell you what happened because the medicine is better and it makes me more able to do something like writing a long book. But back then, things were different.*

*I was put in the state hospital because I beat up a homosexual. They said I was delusional, insane.*

*I was lucky not to be in prison. That's where I'd be today. Today, I'd be killed in prison.*

*Over and over again, the little man kept telling me, "Homosexuality's not the problem, Roy. Rape is."*

*I tell you all this so you'll understand why I was in this hospital. After I wrote this whole story down the first time, I read it, and it occurred to me I told you what had happened, but I made myself seem sane. I made myself and the other people seem like ordinary people.*

*That's just what we pretended to be. Insofar as possible, many of us, not nearly all, wanted to appear normal. But the Sunrise State Hospital was not filled with normal people.*

# 3

## The Catholic Chapel

The next night I slipped through the bakery and over the loading dock to the outside. That allowed me to make my way across the kind of back court area to an outside entrance that led to the tunnels.

The hospital was honeycombed with huge concrete tunnels built back in the 1800s. You could take the elevator to get to the tunnels . . . if you wanted to get caught. Otherwise, you made your way to them through an outside door.

The tunnels had small apartments off of them. They were once living quarters for some of the employees. There was still some old furniture down there—broken-down beds, chairs with the stuffing coming out, and things like that.

There was a small Catholic chapel down there too. It was built in one of the concrete rooms. The altar and all the pews were handmade. The previous priest, who had been there forever, was a master woodworker. He did beautiful work in light oak. There were handmade curlicues around the altar and on the confessional.

I attended church in that chapel, but I didn't take communion. They wouldn't let me. I was Protestant.

The only reason I attended church at all was to be reminded of the hypocrisy of religious people. The most evil man I ever knew went to church each Sunday—in a beautifully proportioned traditional Protestant church. He is the one who gave the money for remodeling his church, but that's another story.

Tonight I went to the chapel because that's what the note told me to do. The note said: "Wednesday in the chapel." It was written in a kind of shaky hand, the kind of handwriting I expected the dead man in the priest suit just might have.

The dead man in the priest suit was a stranger to me. How did he know his way around so well? And how did he get into the record room?

The chapel door was unlocked, which was usual. The priests still saw the chapel as a place for people to come and pray. They didn't lock up like they were supposed to.

As I went in, I saw the tabernacle sitting on the altar up in front. It was also made of wood with a small carving of Jesus on the front. The Catholics thought Jesus lived inside. It's kind of like that old Prince Albert tobacco joke. When we were kids, we'd phone the small corner store and say, "Do you have Prince Albert in a can?" and when they said, "Yes," then we'd say, "Well, you'd better let him out." I always thought the people at the store already knew the joke and just played along.

It always seemed absurd to me to think that people believed Jesus lived in places like that little tabernacle.

At first glance, it didn't seem like there was anybody in the chapel. There were only a few places to hide. The altar was set forward a little with a small robing room behind it. That was for the priest and the altar boys.

And then there was the confessional. That was the most likely place.

I found George Carson in the confessional. He seemed startled when I slipped into the priest's part of the confessional and opened the little door. The first little door was on the empty side, but as I opened the other side I saw George Carson through the latticework, his green eyes looking at me through his horn-rimmed glasses. Then he started to duck out the curtain and slip away. He was a widely built, mustached man who moved awkwardly. His hair was dark. His face had several days' worth of stubble. Unless you caught him off guard, he wouldn't look straight at you. He always avoided your glance. He'd been that way ever since I'd known him.

"Not so fast," I said, stepping out of the booth. He stopped dead in his tracks.

"I didn't expect to find *you* here," he said, not looking directly at me. He muttered to himself. It was a sign of his illness. He was what they called manic, talking to himself and making people up. I don't know if he saw things, but I'd bet he did.

He would sometimes break away from his own conversations to talk to you. Otherwise, he seemed to live in his own world.

I just waited, standing in the doorway of the priest part of the confessional.

"I didn't get the letter," George said. "He told me to be here tonight, but he told me I was supposed to get a letter first."

I must have paused, trying to think what to say. And that pause was just enough to make him suspicious. He stopped in his muttering and looked me over, probably noticing who it was for the first time.

"You're not the one I'm supposed to meet here, are you?" He became more confident as he spoke. He put his hands in his pockets, and he stood up straighter.

"I'm the one," I said.

"No, you aren't," he said adamantly. "You don't even know what this is all about." And before I could say anything more, he just turned, walked down the aisle and out the chapel door.

# 4

## The Mail Room

It took a long time to search through the mailbags. They had been brought from town earlier in the day and not dumped and sorted yet. Must have been a busy day.

I didn't often go to the mail room. It was on the first floor of the administration building, in a sort of public front office.

One time the little man came up to me and said, "I know you think Roy Rogers can go anywhere, but stay out of the mail room. Tampering with mail is a federal offense."

I never did know how he knew I had been in the mail room. I was always careful not to leave signs. In some ways, the little man seemed to know everything.

Anyway, tonight, the only thing I knew to do was to dump the sacks of mail, one at a time, on the floor, sort through them, and then put them back together.

I found not one but three letters with the same handwriting as the note. One was to George Carson. Another was to Hoss Jackson, the blacksmith. And the third was to a woman called Nevaeh. I knew her just a little, and I knew that was her only name.

I took all three of the letters, but I didn't open them right then. Instead I went back to the record room. It was more lighted and more private there.

To my surprise, the record room was filled with my delusions. They seemed to gather around the spot where I found the priest-suited man. They came at me, but I had taken my medicine, and I was strong tonight.

"You hover over evil," I told them. It might have sounded kind of grandiose, but it was true. They hovered over evil places, and they seemed to come at me from evil places.

I stared them down, and they started to recede, but I knew they were still there. Still, it felt good to have mastered them, at least this time, and to be able to settle down at the little desk and do my work.

All three envelopes had old clippings in them. The clippings were all the same. They were yellowed and brittle. They were brief. Whoever sent them must have had a lot of copies of the old *Sunrise Sentinel* for that date. None of the clippings was dated.

"Body Found in Local Church," the headline said. "The body of Marcia Weinhart of Sunrise was found last night on the altar of St. Adrienne's Roman Catholic Church," the story went on. "According to Police Chief Homer Steinberg, Mrs. Weinhart was 'killed by foul play.' The chief refused to elaborate," the story said.

*Mrs. Weinhart was widowed and lived alone at 334 Pine Tree Avenue in Sunrise. She was an active member of St. Adrienne's Church, often involved in activities there. According to her former pastor, Father Mitchell Coonie, "She was a wonderful and saintly woman. It is hard to visualize who might have done this to her."*

*The Sentinel will provide further details when they are available.*

And that was all.

The name Marcia Weinhart seemed familiar to me, but I couldn't remember why.

Later that night, I told Harry about finding George Carson in the chapel, but I didn't tell him about stealing the letters from the mail room. That was not the kind of thing you ever shared.

"I wonder who told George to go to the chapel?" I said.

"I don't know," Harry answered. I had expected him to say that maybe it had been the little man.

When I talked to George Carson the next day, he refused to say anything. He just turned away, muttering to himself, and I knew there was nothing I could do to make him talk.

"We need witnesses," Harry said later. "That would make him talk."

"Witnesses. What do you mean?"

"I used to listen to Philip Marlowe on the radio," Harry said. Harry was different from me. He didn't have delusions. He was more what they now call mentally handicapped, though I never saw that.

"I thought Philip Marlowe was a character in a book."

"I can't read," Harry said. "I heard him on the radio. It was a few years back. There was a Philip Marlowe episode called 'Life Can Be Murder.' Philip met this woman who it looked like killed somebody. By that time, she had slipped away from him and he couldn't find her. He went to the place she worked, at least that's what I remember, and he sweet-talked her boss into telling where she lived and what her phone number was.

"There was a barkeeper named Belle. She led Marlowe to the boss.

"Belle and the boss were witnesses, people who tell you about something they saw or who lead you somewhere else. Every mystery story needs its witnesses."

"This is not a story, Harry."

"But it's all the same," he said.

"No, it's not," I said. "The only witness to this man's death is the one who killed him. We can't ask anybody else about it. They don't even know he's dead."

"All mystery stories need their witnesses," Harry said stubbornly. "We'll need a witness too. You just wait and see. We'll need a witness."

# 5

## The Blacksmith Shop

### THURSDAY, JANUARY 7, 1954

Thursday I had three short, kind of unproductive conversations. The first was at the blacksmith shop. To me, the blacksmith shop was one of the most interesting places in the whole hospital complex. It was on the "back lot," so to speak. We had passed it as we took the body to be buried.

It had that burned-iron smell you always get in places like that, but even more, there were rusty tools hanging on the wall and scraps of iron lying around. You could look up and see the network of leather belts used to help run the bellows that stoked the forge. Some of the belts also ran the grinders. Originally this was done with foot pedals, which were pumped to move the belts and make things work, but in an age of electricity the foot pedals were gone now.

A huge brick fireplace sat against one wall.

The blacksmith shop was partitioned into two rooms—one huge one that would hold several wagons and another just as wide but much shallower where the blacksmith did the finer work.

Today, the big swinging doors of the large room were closed. It was cold outside, and there was only one wooden wagon sitting on the inside. It had a broken leaf spring on a back wheel.

One afternoon last summer, Harry and I spent several hours watching Hoss nail large shoes on Pat and Mike. Most often, the horses were gentle and accepting. The mules were usually a different matter. They would bite you in a New York minute.

Hoss was a poor interview. The most I'd ever heard him say was, "They don't need blacksmiths as much anymore."

Hoss was a gray-balding man with wire glasses. He wasn't young anymore. He limped from the damage done by numerous animal kicks over the years. Still, he just kept swinging the hammer without saying much.

The rumor around the hospital was that he had killed a man. Hoss was found to be insane, the rumor said, but those who knew him weren't so sure.

Hoss was a huge man, strong, with bulging biceps, the kind of person you would visualize when you read the poem "The Village Blacksmith," except he had a huge potbelly. I never visualized the village blacksmith with a huge potbelly.

There wasn't any social talk with Hoss. You either watched in silence or, if you asked something, got a one-word or one-line answer. He was always that way.

"Did you know someone named Marcia Weinhart?" I asked.

"No."

"Even years ago."

"I don't talk about years ago."

"What if it is important?"

"I don't talk about years ago."

"Suppose it is a life-and-death matter?"

"No," he said. And that was it. If I had to depend upon talking to Hoss to learn something about Marcia Weinhart, I'd never learn it. But with Hoss, I thought, there was another way. It would take a little longer, but there was another way.

Nevaeh was a bit more loquacious.

When I first knew Nevaeh, she had been beaten up. She had two black eyes. I met her right after she had come to the hospital. She had had a fight with someone on the ward.

"I got the best of it," she said.

"They didn't gig you in some way?" I asked her. It was the usual thing to discipline someone for fighting.

"They knew what happened. The old . . . ," and she used a nasty word. "The old bulls on the ward surrounded me and took me on. They wanted to show me who was boss."

"But you showed them."

"I showed them," she said. She smiled a kind of gap-toothed smile. If she hadn't had such a hard life, she would have been a beautiful young woman. Some of her beauty still shined through.

There wasn't a lot of fighting, but there was some. I guess there's no way around it.

"You were gonna get a letter that had a clipping in it, an old clipping from the newspaper about the death of a woman named Marcia Weinhart," I told Nevaeh when I saw her this time. I didn't know her very well at all, but after Hoss, I decided to be more direct. If someone called me on it, I could always lie.

Nevaeh and I were walking on the hospital grounds. The grounds were her usual haunt.

"She took me in one time when I was twelve years old," Nevaeh said. "She was a nice lady."

"Took you in?"

"I was homeless. I've been homeless since I was born." By this time, Nevaeh was a young woman, maybe in her mid-thirties at the most. She had the most beautiful teeth with a small gap right in the bottom center. That made her different from almost anyone I knew here.

They had a good dentist here. He worked only at the hospital, not in town. But by the time he got most of us, our teeth were shot. I never understood how Nevaeh's teeth could have been so perfect.

Nevaeh's ratty black hair surrounded a still young-looking but worn face. You could almost visualize her when she was just a child.

"Your name means 'heaven,' " I said. "It's the word 'heaven' spelled backward."

"My mother's sick little joke. I was born under a bridge in Kansas City. That's the god-awful truth. She never even went to a hospital or a whatever you call them women who deliver babies.

"She named me Heaven because I was born in hell."

I was floored.

"This is almost the best place I ever lived," she said. "They feed me. They have soft beds."

"But they don't protect you from the fighters," I said.

"That don't matter now," she said. "Once the fighters learn you can hold your own, they leave you alone."

"What else can you tell me about Marcia Weinhart?"

"Not now. I won't tell you now," she said.

"What does that mean?"

"I won't tell you now. I don't know you. I need to see your references."

"Talk to Harry," I told Nevaeh. "He'll give you the particulars." And we each went our separate ways.

When I got back to the ward, there was a note that a tough, middle-aged patient named Alice wanted to see me out on the grounds. Patients passed notes all the time, especially between the men and women. If you came back and found your pillow arranged in a certain way, you knew there was a note under it. Someone had gotten someone on the ward to bring it.

Alice was one of the bulls who had tried to beat up Nevaeh and failed.

"Stay away from George Carson," Alice told me. She was a dumpy, dark, masculine-faced woman with short, bowl-cut, dark hair. In a way, she was also one of the most dangerous people in the hospital. One time, she accused the kitchen staff of food poisoning. She wrote letters to government officials. There was an investigation.

It turned out the whole thing was a hoax, but state officials still came barreling in. I knew she must have some kind of pull, or people thought she did. Otherwise she would have been ignored. I know people who have written about real things, and they are never listened to.

"What's it to you if I talk to George?" I asked.

"He's a friend of mine," she said. She probably fancied herself to be George Carson's girlfriend. One of the common delusions of psychotic women is that someone is in love with them, maybe even going to marry them. Sometimes those delusionary lovers are people who are dead or they are even famous people.

Alice and George as a couple, that was hard to visualize, but I could believe he had encouraged her to think it could be so. George knew how to work people.

I started to walk away.

"I'll tell them I saw you carrying someone's record."

I turned back.

"You break into the record room. You know you do. Most people don't know it, but I do. I'll tell them you had a record on the ward or somewhere else where I could see it. You were showing parts around. You were sharing confidential information."

"You'd have to prove it."

"The great thing about accusations is that they cause an awful lot of trouble, whether or not you prove them, and they sometimes stick," she said. "I learned that from a friend of mine, a politician."

"Two can play the game, Alice," I said, looking directly at her. She squirmed. She didn't like people who looked right at her. The only time she looked anyone in the eye was to intimidate. "Whatever I do to you, I won't announce it beforehand. And it won't necessarily come from me, but I promise you, when it happens you'll be here forever."

She flinched. Not ever getting out of here was her greatest fear. She hated being in this place, and she hated all of us who saw it as the best we could do. She was always talking about how she was going to get out, how there had been some huge mistake that put her here. She was a strange lady. Some days you would see her and she seemed just as normal as possible. And other days you'd think the sun and all the stars had gotten together to conspire against her. I think they call it intermittent paranoia, at least now, but the truth is, if you are truly paranoid, you can do terrible things that seem logical considering the way you see the world.

In some ways, Alice was a dangerous person.

"Just stay away from George," she said, and then she left.

She didn't have to worry. I'd already talked to George, and he had given me the silent treatment.

# 6

## On the Ward

I t was after eight in the evening. The whole horde was in the gathering room looking at the little black-and-white TV set. I just stood back and watched them. I could hear Groucho Marx's voice coming from among the circled chairs and standing men. He was asking his still silly question about who is buried in Grant's tomb.

When I glanced away from the group I saw the little man pedaling across the ward looking straight at me. He worked all the time. He always went triple speed, and he always took stairs three at a time. His expensive suits and flashy ties made him stand out.

"We've got a problem, Roy," he told me when he got there.

"Oh."

"Harry stole a bouquet of flowers and put it in a horse's stall."

"Oh."

"I don't want to know about this, do I?" he said.

"Probably not."

"Anyway," the little man said, "one of the attendants brought a bouquet of roses to work with her. It was special, something she received on her engagement. You know how that is?"

"I've never been engaged," I said, and he just smiled at me. He knew my tricks.

"Get off it," he said. "Harry stole the flowers, put them in the horse's stall, and the horse trampled on them before she ate the tops off. Now the young lady's about to have a mental breakdown."

"I'll talk to Harry."

"Tell him to stay away from that young lady for a while."

"I thought I would."

But he wasn't done yet: "I told her I'd buy her another bouquet," he said, "and she just shouted, 'Sure, and then I can press *your* flowers in my memory book, and fifty years from now I can tell my grandchildren about the time their father and I got engaged and some nut at the mental institution where I worked took the flowers Buck gave me and put them where a horse could trample them, and then the superintendent of the place bought new flowers for me.'"

"She sounds upset."

"She didn't even stop to take a breath," he said excitedly. "She just went on, 'And then I can tell them, with true emotion in my heart and voice, "These flowers mean so much to me. They remind me of the horse's ass I worked for back in 1954."'"

"You're too easy on them," I replied.

That set him back. He actually stopped talking.

"She knows you won't fire her for calling you a horse's ass."

"Actually, after that, I told her, 'Well, it would make a pretty good story,' and we both broke down laughing. Finally, she said, 'You can buy more flowers if you want. After all, they're just flowers.'"

" 'Everybody's got some good in them,' " I said, quoting what he often said to me. Personally I didn't believe it, but I'm almost sure he did. He used to say all kind of things like that, things like, "Nothing lasts forever," and, "Never forget, people are more important than things."

"Tell Harry to quit putting flowers in the horse's stall."

"I thought I would. Somehow it seems so untoward."

"Roy Rogers always has the answer," he told me with a smile. He was a smart man. He had my number. One time he told me jokingly, "You don't fool me. I don't really think you think you're Roy Rogers, but if that's your dodge, it's OK with me."

When I just acted puzzled, he got a serious look on his face and said, "Let me tell you something, Roy. There's an ethics to this 'crazy' thing. There's 'crazy' and there's 'bad.' It's OK to be 'crazy.' In fact, a whole lot of people probably are. But 'bad' is a different matter. It's not right to use your 'crazy' to cover up your 'bad.' "

Before he could go on, I shot back at him, ". . . and the attorney asked, 'Does the defendant know the difference between right and wrong?' "

"You've got it," he said. "Roy Rogers always stands for justice. It's OK for you to think you're Roy Rogers as long as you believe in justice."

And I almost cried, except I wouldn't let him see how close he'd come to knowing why I chose to be Roy Rogers.

"You've got to quit putting flowers in Pat's stall," I told Harry when we were alone later that evening.

"That priest man deserves to be remembered too," Harry said.

"We don't want him remembered. We want him forgotten. You can't tell anyone about him, Harry."

"I won't tell. But still, he deserves to be remembered."

"There's a whole graveyard of forgotten people, Harry. They just have numbered markers. Go out there and remember them." There was no reasoning with Harry. There was just diverting him to something else. "But don't go stealing flowers to do it," I said quickly. "Stealing flowers only draws attention to us."

"I had to steal them. It's January. We ain't got no flowers now."

"Sign up for crafts. Go over there to the big brick building by the lake and let them teach you how to draw pictures of flowers or make little flowers out of clay. It's called recreational therapy, Harry. They think it helps to heal you."

"OK," he said, and I just smiled. I had to wonder how long it would be before I saw the little man pedaling across the ward again. This time he would say, "We've got a problem, Roy. Harry's put all kinds of pictures of flowers on our unmarked graves."

## Another Personal Note

*The little man was always asking me why I attacked the man I attacked. I never told him.*

*He said he didn't really have to know, but he was interested. He said he thought it had something to do with why I was Roy Rogers.*

*Have you ever watched the Roy Rogers movies? Much of the time Roy gets branded as the bad guy. He is the guy who stole the horses or who robbed the stagecoach.*

*Of course, it didn't happen that way. There was always a misunderstanding that made him look like the bad guy. When the thing was all over, Roy Rogers was the one who brought peace and sanity to the world.*

One time, I told the little man, "I used to beat fags."

He was quite disturbed. " 'Fags.' That's a hate term, Roy. That's the kind of language people use when they want to kill someone. Roy Rogers wouldn't use a word like that."

And that's when I began to really change.

# 7

## At the Little Store

The next day, I made my way down the steps from the left wing of the building. Out in front of the administration building there was a vast expanse. You crossed the street, and then there were several blocks of green vacant land.

They weren't exactly vacant. For one thing, in the far distant left corner, they had the most beautiful cyprus trees I've ever seen. They were carefully maintained by a gardener who, by now, was a seemingly ancient man, truly probably close to eighty. He still puttered around the place, his back bent, his straw hat on his head, planting trees and bushes. It was his vocation.

There was one long sidewalk that split the plot in half. You could walk straight out the administration building, across the street, and down the sidewalk until finally you came to a county road. On the other side of the county road was the Sunrise baseball field. If you turned left and went about half a block, you came to Sheridan's, the little store.

Sheridan's was privately owned. It was a kind of combination gas station, store, and bar. The family owned quite a lot of land in that part of town. The little store was probably there because patients sometimes walked down and spent their money there. Patients had money from their families. Sometimes they could keep from having it confiscated and put in the canteen fund, but that only happened if their families gave it to them cash in hand.

Also, hospital employees might have stopped at the little store on the way home too.

John Sheridan, the store's owner, would let me use the phone for local calls.

I called Nancy Jane in town. She was a volunteer, only in her twenties, who had become a friend. She worked the patient dances in the evenings and sometimes on the weekends, helping oversee the music and the people.

We got to talking one day, and I think she found me interesting. "You're a lot smarter than you look," she told me.

I didn't reply. Roy Rogers is humble if he's anything at all.

Anyway, once in a while, Nancy Jane would do things in town that I needed to have done. When I got her on the phone, I told her, "There was a murder sometime back in Sunrise."

"A murder?"

"The lady's name was Marcia Weinhart. She was found murdered inside St. Adrienne's Catholic Church."

"Why would you need to know about a murder?"

"I need to know when that happened. I've seen a little clipping about it, probably the first story printed, but it didn't have a date on it."

"Why . . . ?"

"Also, I need to see copies of any other stories that followed that one."

"You're not gonna tell me, are you?" she said. "Why you need to know, I mean."

"No."

"But you do really need to know?"

"I do really need to know. It's more important than I can tell you now."

"*The Sentinel* is open Saturdays till noon. I'll try to get there as soon as they open tomorrow. If I find anything, I'll make a visit Sunday afternoon."

"Sounds good to me," I said. She was a great blessing to me. There were a lot of things we didn't get in trouble for—we being me and the other trusted patients like me. But going into town would get you in big trouble indeed.

The town was hypocritical. It soaked up the salaries that the mental institution produced. This place was the major employer in the whole county, probably providing more than most of the other entities put together, but still the town was ashamed of us.

We were out at the edge of town with a long winding concrete road leading up to the main building. Originally there had been a fence around the place with an arched metal gate at the entrance. There were all kinds of jokes about patients standing at that fence and saying different things to passersby.

The fence and gate were gone by the 1950s.

One time some rich guy in Sunrise gave Sunrise money to make a history mural in the city hall. When the mural was unveiled, it didn't have any picture of the insane asylum. Here it was, the major employer in the whole county for more than half a century, and the people didn't even acknowledge it as a part of county history.

So we patients didn't try to sneak into town. If you did that, all hell broke loose.

When I got back from the store, I talked to George Carson again. "Alice talked to me about you," I told him.

"She thinks she loves me," he said.

33

"And you encourage her."

"I can't stand her. I would never touch her, but I don't tell her that I hate her either."

"She can get us all in trouble," I replied.

"Not me," he said. "You maybe, but not me."

"She knows more than I might expect her to," I said.

"She doesn't know as much as she thinks she does," George said. "I told her too much once. I won't do that again . . . ," and then he added the words, ". . . with anybody."

I tried to get him to say more, but he wouldn't.

# 8

## On the Ward

Saturday night, I had this terrible urge to go out to Hoss' old tree, but I knew I couldn't do it. He might be there. He went there most of all on weekends. I'd have to wait till late Monday afternoon or night to go there, so I just hung around the ward and talked to Harry.

# 9

><+<◆>~+<>~<◆>+<⊰

# The Willow Tree

On Sunday, I went to church and then waited on the ward.

Like I told you, I went to church to remind myself of the evil in the world, all those holier-than-thou people doing terrible things to their friends and family and then going to church to be forgiven. At least that's how it seemed to me.

Church was one place the delusions didn't follow me. The priest talked in a language I didn't understand, and even though he gave his sermon in English, he just prattled on, but still there was a peace about it. Even when the faceless rapists had held me down the night before and tried to force me—I never let them do it—they were put to rest at church.

It wasn't that way for everybody. Sometimes I watched the little man go over and sit beside people who were talking to themselves a mile a minute. He would whisper to the person, usually one woman in particular, and the priest would just go on as if nothing had happened.

I've even watched the little man walk up to take communion, holding the prattling woman by the hand. When it came time to take communion, she stopped babbling and kneeled like the rest and took communion.

I didn't take communion. They wouldn't let me. I wasn't Catholic.

Sometimes at church I thought about Roy Rogers and his family. I read everything I could about Roy and Dale. They faced a lot of unhappiness, children who died in difficult circumstances. But still, I always felt there was a kind of peace about them. I could visualize them with their family around the dinner table, and it was different from the dinner table I had known at my home.

Everything I read and knew about Roy Rogers and Dale Evans made me think they knew something special about living. That's why I chose to be Roy Rogers, and as I look back on it, I know I have never regretted the choice.

After church, I went to lunch with the other patients in the patient cafeteria. Usually we had a light meal at Sunday noon, something not so hard to prepare because there was probably less staff on weekends.

When Nancy Jane came, I met her in the visiting room. "Let's go outside," I said.

"It'll be cold out there," she said. She was a thin-faced lady with a huge smile and brownish red hair.

"You're bundled up and so am I," I said.

We walked awhile and then sat on a bench in front of the willow tree across the street from the administration building. During the summer, if you wanted to hide, you could go into the dome formed by the weeping willow tree and no one would think to find you there.

"This is really serious," she said. She was shivering.

I didn't say anything.

"You don't want anyone to overhear us. Well, let's get it over with and get back inside."

"What did you find out?"

"You tapped into Sunrise's great unsolved murder. When I asked the editor of *The Sentinel*—a man with a great mop of white hair—he said, 'Oh my God! Why do you want to know about all that?'

"Marcia Weinhart was murdered in May of 1934," she said. "There was that initial clipping, and not much else except an obituary. It was so sensitive they didn't write another news story about it. The present editor of *The Sentinel* told me most everything I know.

"When he asked why I wanted to know, I just told him I'd had a friend inquire."

" 'You can't keep things quiet,' he said, 'even after twenty years.'

"He went on to say they found her body on the altar. He even showed me a picture they had taken at the time but never used. The picture was sharp and glaring, the way they are when you use those old press cameras with their four-by-five negatives and bright flashes.

"She had been stabbed at least a hundred times. That was clear from just one glance.

" 'The cops put the clamp on it,' he told me. He had been a young reporter back then. 'I wanted to do more with it, but the publisher wouldn't let me. Someone was sure interested in it. As soon as that first story ran, someone went around and stole all the papers from the local sale boxes. We had to do a second run.'

" 'You had the picture in your middle drawer,' I told him, and he flushed a little, and then said, 'I keep this picture to remind me. There's a story which we haven't told,' and then he smiled. 'But without help, I could never flesh it out.'

" 'I can't promise you I'll help you tell it,' I told him.

" 'But, maybe . . . ,' he replied.

"I copied the obituary for you," Nancy Jane said, handing me a couple spiral-tablet pages with her handwriting on it. "Now let's go inside."

Once we got inside, we played dominoes for several games. I even let her win a couple, just because.

# 10

# Hoss' Tree

Of all the things I'm going to tell you about in this little history, I'm most ashamed of this. No one had ever gone to Hoss' tree. It was his. It was a large oak tree with a huge hollow in it. Hoss went out and stuffed papers in it.

It was back behind the recreational therapy building in a little grove of trees.

One time, the little man told me the story of how a small gray squirrel tried to take over Hoss' hollow tree. The squirrel got in the hole and just started bailing, sending paper everywhere. When Hoss found his papers all over the ground, some of them blown away, he stuffed the ones he could find back into the hole. The squirrel came again. Hoss stuffed the papers back.

This happened several times, and then Hoss staked out the tree. When he saw the squirrel, he decided he had to do something about it. He tried to sneak a .22 rifle onto the grounds through a friend. Hoss was caught and got into a lot of trouble.

When he finally told the little man what was happening, the

little man arranged with the conservation department to trap the squirrel and take it away, so Hoss got back his tree. I've always thought they probably put some kind of repellent there to keep more squirrels away.

"It must have been a crazy squirrel," the conservation department told the little man. "Most squirrels wouldn't have anything to do with things so full of human smell."

No one ever knew what Hoss put in his tree. He'd been doing it for years. They just knew Hoss was quiet and troubled. He worked almost without speaking. He had supposedly killed a man once. No one knew for sure if that was true. If it was, it had to be one of those cases where he was found to be insane and put in an asylum. He was probably also considered pretty safe, since there was another hospital in another place that was supposedly for the criminally insane.

Everyone saw shoeing horses as Hoss' salvation, the one thing he could do to keep the demons away.

Even when he was facing his demons, and we all did, he did it in a different way. He got quieter and quieter. No one knew exactly what his demons were, whether they were threatening figures like mine were, family portraits that somehow haunted him, or some kind of ethereal spirits of the kind that so often flitted in and out of people's minds in places such as this. Hoss never said, probably even to the little man.

Sometimes the most debilitating thing was black depression. There weren't any figures connected with it. There was simply blackness. Somehow I had always thought that such depression haunted Hoss.

So now here it was, almost ten o'clock in the morning, and I was going out to Hoss' tree.

Hoss would have been working at that time of day. Besides, he didn't go to the tree except at night. Almost everyone knew he went out to the tree, but he thought his trips were some kind of secret. He wasn't supposed to be out at the usual times he went, but what the heck, I usually was out when I wasn't supposed to be out at those times either.

I found the old hole stuffed full of papers. Many of the existing letters were old and cracking, and God only knows how much of the debris in the bottom of the hollow was from decayed letters. Hoss' pencil drawings were among the papers.

I didn't know Hoss could draw, but as it turns out, he was quite a good artist. The very clear and detailed drawings were of some man raping a little boy. You could see the child's pants down around his ankles. The different drawings showed the scene from several different angles. It was as if Hoss drew it over and over again.

In every case, the man's face was just a blank circle, but the little boy had a name on him—Hoss.

That afternoon, I visited the Sunrise community cemetery across from the hospital. You remember how I said you could walk down the sidewalk that split the large tract across the street from the administration building? At the end of the sidewalk was the Sunrise baseball field. And over to the right about a quarter of a mile was one of the Sunrise cemeteries.

According to the obituary I had from Nancy Jane, Marcia Weinhart was buried there. That's why I walked over there.

I like to never found the grave, it was so nondescript.

When I did find it, it was a single grave—not in a family plot. The family plot would have been in the Catholic cemetery. For generations on end, her whole family had been devout Catholics. The Catholic cemetery would be filled with Weinharts.

Not only was she buried alone, but she was over at the edge, by the paupers' graves, the graves where they buried the occasional wayfarer or other unnamed person who happened to be so unkind as to die in Sunrise.

The placing of the pauper graves was very clear. At the center of the cemetery was a stone chapel. It wasn't used anymore. In fact, it was supposed to be locked, but I could get in. When you went inside, you found a few old pews, a little stone altar at the front, and mildew on the walls. But the building had clearly been the centerpiece of the whole layout.

If you drew a diagonal from the southeast to the northwest corner of the original cemetery straight through the little building, you would have the longest distance in the cemetery. The paupers' graves were in the southeast corner, as far away from the main building and as far off the beaten cemetery paths as possible.

The paupers were not only set off to the side. They were almost hidden, with the hope they'd be forgotten.

If you had wanted to insult Marcia Weinhart, to slap her in the face, you couldn't have done it any better than to have buried her where she was buried. Back then, the Catholics were serious about their cemeteries. If you were divorced or had been proven to have committed adultery, you weren't buried in the Catholic cemetery unless you were rich or had some special pull. Only the real congregation, the real "holier-than-thou" types, could be buried in the Catholic cemetery.

Even then, the Catholic cemetery had its rank. I had gone to the funeral of the old priest who did all the woodwork. All the priests and nuns who had died in Sunrise or who wanted to be buried in Sunrise were buried in one section, three or four rows deep, clear across the whole west end of the cemetery. Their heads were to the west so when they rose again they'd be facing Jesus, who was coming from the east. The priests were buried in one row. The nuns from the convent in the town were buried back behind them, still in rank as they always were. And then the town itself was out in front of the clergy, in the eastern two-thirds of the cemetery. They were the congregation, so to speak.

There were so many priests and nuns because there had been a semilarge convent in Sunrise, a house for nuns. They had had an orphanage there. When that went by the wayside, the mother-house and all the other buildings remained, but most of the nuns went out to teach in Catholic schools around the state.

If you were a Catholic, walking through the Sunrise Catholic cemetery was a bit like walking through the Catholic segment of the town back when you were alive. All your old friends were there.

It wasn't quite that way with the Protestant cemeteries. For one thing, there were more than one of them and the town was large enough that when you divided it up between two or three major cemeteries and God knows how many smaller ones, you divided up the friends too. But only the real outcasts were buried where Marcia Weinhart was buried.

"They didn't like you much, did they?" I said to Marcia, and it was as if I could hear her saying, "No, they didn't."

I wanted to ask her why they didn't like her, but I guessed that she wouldn't tell me. She would say, "The townspeople have kept it all among themselves. Why should I spread the story around now?" And she would know there was very little chance I'd ever find out.

But she didn't know Roy Rogers. Roy Rogers was committed to the truth, to justice and fairness and goodness. Nothing deterred him from that. After all, if the world is going to be the kind of world it should be, not the kind of world it is, we should all be Roy Rogers—or Dale Evans. They were a team, you know.

"I'll find out your story," I told Marcia Weinhart as I turned to go back to the hospital. "In fact, my finding out has already begun."

# 11

><=+=<⊛=+=○=+=⊛=+=<⊡=

# The Record Room

Just before midnight on Monday night, I slipped down to the record room and looked up Nevaeh. There was no birth certificate. In fact, there was a note in the little man's handwriting: "Homeless. No birth certificate of any kind. Indeterminate name and age."

There were no medical records from before she came. Even the least of us usually had some kind of medical records.

> *Parents unknown [the record said]. Patient says her mother was an alcoholic who abandoned her at eight years old. 'Fifty-one flood flushed her out from around the KC stockyards. Police had her committed here.*
>
> *Histoplasmosis, non-disseminated. Signs of frequent pneumonia. She had pneumonia when she came here.*
>
> *Claims to have no knowledge of her family. One special friend she roamed with, but that woman was a Negro.*

The last note was an indication of the fact that the Sunrise State Hospital had not yet been integrated. When they did integrate state hospitals, Sunrise was one of the first because Missouri is a southern state and mental health officials knew the little man could deal with the crap integration would bring.

The little man felt about Negroes much as he felt about homosexuals. They were just people to be accepted like other people. The little man himself was born of immigrants. He was probably raised in poverty, at least to begin with. He knew what it was to be among the left out, to live in poor conditions. I don't think he ever forgot that.

It was that night, the night I looked up Nevaeh's records, that I first became fully aware of the importance of the record room. For some people, their whole histories were in that place. The record room would become the crown jewel of the hospital. At the time, I just had an inkling of how important the record room would become, but even as recently as just four years ago, in 1992, I had someone learn I had been a patient in the hospital. They came to the nursing home to ask me if I knew who could tell them what happened to the records.

I just said, "No." I didn't tell them about the record room or that I was often in there. I certainly didn't tell them I had rummaged through the records.

I did do one thing, though. I wrote this book. I wrote it for my own people. They might not ever get to see the records. I don't even know if the records survived. But they can know my record. Records are important. That's why the hospital had a record room.

The record room seemed to be about half a block square. It was rows and rows of file cabinets, and each of the cabinets had these file folders. There were other things too, things like the plat of the hospital cemetery.

The records themselves had all kinds of things in them, a mug-shot type picture of the person (the hospital had its own part-time photographer), referral letters, records from other institutions (occasionally prisons), and written medical notes. There were even historical pictures and things like that.

One time I found the record of a man who had tried to "run away." Several people a year tried to do that. There in the little man's rounded, fairly large handwriting was the note: "Informed sheriff and called family." And then, a dated and timed note written just a couple hours later: "Found John hiding behind a rose trellis at my house. Said he didn't have anyplace else to go. Authorities and family notified."

John's words always stuck with me as the most profound words in the records I'd read. The little man's house was on the grounds of the hospital, just about a block or so away from the main building. John was like a lot of us. He didn't have anyplace else to go.

When they closed those institutions and tore down the buildings—most of them are gone now—I just wanted to shout, "Those were people nobody wanted. They were abandoned old folks with dementia, people with certifiable mental illnesses, and God knows who else."

There were also some *One Flew over the Cuckoo's Nest* types, but even among those, most were just throwaways, including me.

When they closed those institutions and tried to deal with the crazy folks in other ways, the whole system went to hell. Today, almost every week, you read another story about the deplorable condition of the treatment of mentally ill in this state.

There is newspaper story after newspaper story of mental health money going unused or being siphoned off for other things.

Of course, I'm biased. I liked the place. I found a role there. Not everyone did, and many hated it.

I'm not stupid. I know some mental hospitals did terrible things to patients, but that wasn't the way it was at Sunrise when I was there.

Finally, society has to decide. Now, most of us are homeless, living under bridges and getting the hell beat out of us just for the fun of it by gangs of crazy teenagers. Is that a better way? Finally, the people choose.

Of all the places in that whole huge institution, I came to feel the two most important places were the record room and the cemetery. The time would come when they held all that was left of I-have-no-idea-how-many-thousand people.

# 12

# On the Ward

## TUESDAY AFTERNOON, JANUARY 12, 1954

gain, I saw the little man coming across the ward toward me. He obviously had something on his mind.

"Harry has a puppy under his bed," he said to me when he got me away from the crowd.

"Good for Harry."

"You know we can't have that. I know how Harry feels about animals, but we can't let him have a puppy on the ward."

"Take it away and he'll just get another one."

"I've done all kinds of things for Harry," the little man said. "I got him the job cleaning out the horses' stalls, and he tries to leave them flowers. Now he's hiding a dog under his bed."

"Maybe we could build a doghouse out around the barn."

"And let Harry keep the puppy there," the little man replied. He was considering it.

"It wouldn't work," the little man said finally. "We'd have to get the dog its vaccinations and get it neutered or spayed—I don't even know what kind of dog it is."

"You worry too much about little things."

"If we keep it, getting that dog taken care of is important."

I heard the "if we keep it," so I didn't argue with him. He was gradually going to come around.

"I've got an employee, Kurt Harrison, who's raising hell about Harry having a dog."

"He raises hell about everything. He doesn't like me and Harry. He thinks we're troublemakers. He's one of your fundamentally fine people who's not so fundamentally fine." The little man was always saying about someone, "No matter what he's done, I'm sure he's a fundamentally fine person." Sometimes I wanted to tell him that some people just aren't "fundamentally fine."

The little man seemed to stop and think a minute. Then he shook his head. "We can't do it," he said finally. "Half the patients in the place might like to have a pet. We just can't do it."

And that was that. The little man was a good man, but he could be hardheaded too. "I'll give you two days to get the dog out of there without . . ." He paused.

"Without what?"

"Without upsetting Harry." The little man smiled and then walked away. He knew what he was asking me to do. Find a way to let Harry keep the dog. Harry wouldn't be happy any other way. But find that way without anyone around the hospital knowing what was happening. In other words, go around the rules, but don't let the authorities know it, and the little man was the "authorities."

Well, his wish was my command, so I set out to do it.

# 13

## In the Auditorium

I think the Roy Rogers movies are a hoot and a howl.

Tonight it was *The Cowboy and the Senorita.* I knew I'd better enjoy it because there wouldn't be any more Roy Rogers movies for a while.

"People are getting tired of Roy Rogers," the little man had told me earlier that day. "They think we're having Roy just a bit too much."

So this would be the last one for a while, but it was a good one. Roy and his sidekick Big Boy Williams escaped from the bad guys by swinging on the chandeliers. Big Boy was so huge, the chandelier fell with him, and then all the bad guys slipped and fell on chandelier parts.

The judge tried to talk on the phone with a cigar in his mouth, but that was after good had been restored and Roy had proved that Craig Allen was trying to steal the gold mine with all its riches.

This was Roy's first movie with the woman who would become his second wife, Dale Evans. His first wife died after the birth of their son, Dusty, and then Dale came along. Dale's the one who wrote "Happy Trails," their theme song, but that wasn't in this movie.

Even in the Roy Rogers movies, the world is filled with evil. There are people like Craig Allen trying to steal gold mines from unsuspecting helpless victims. Still, underneath it all, there is a current of good, and that current is Roy Rogers and Dale Evans.

For me, at least, the only problem with *The Cowboy and the Senorita* is that it ends with a whole bunch of minutes of singing. It's like it wasn't long enough and they just added to it at the end. But what kind of a critic am I? After all, I'm Roy Rogers, so I'm not unbiased.

"Roy's still alive," the little man told me one time. "And if he's still alive, how can you be Roy Rogers?"

"The one on the screen's an imposter," I told him. "I'm the real one. I just let that other guy play me."

The little man only laughed. He thought I was the imposter. He thought he knew what was happening to me and what had happened, but he didn't. He really didn't.

One time he told me, "It's good that you gain strength from Roy Rogers. But someday, you're going to have to break away and be yourself."

Of course, the little man was wrong.

# 14

# After the Movie

TUESDAY, JANUARY 12, 1954

W e need to go out tonight," I told Harry as we were going back up to the ward.

Harry knew that meant meeting me in the auditorium when he could get away.

"We need to get a doghouse," I told him when he came. "They know you have a dog under the bed, and they aren't going to let you keep it."

"A doghouse? Where?" Harry asked.

"Let's try the carpenter shop. They sometimes make them there." The occupational therapy people made them to sell to the public.

There were two parts to the carpenter shop. There was the "hospital" part, so to speak, where the professional, hired carpenters worked. They did repairs around the buildings and the farm. Then there was the occupational therapy part. That's the part where the patients made things to sell. The sale of items helped pay for the materials they used.

The "hospital" part of the carpenter shop was where they

had all the power tools, the saws and routers and things like that. It smelled like sawdust.

The other part only had regular tools like hammers. It wasn't a separate room. It was a locked, cordoned-off section surrounded by gray metal latticework walls. When the occupational therapy had power tool work to be done, the regular carpenters did it or some trusted patients went back to the power tools and did it under supervision. The other patients just did the putting together.

Anyway, the carpenter shop was over by the little lake, in the same building with the recreational therapy, the radio broadcast studio, and things like that.

But they didn't have any doghouses at the time.

"I'm glad," Harry told me. "I don't like stealing."

"But we still need a doghouse," I replied.

"There's no place else," Harry said.

"Oh yes, there is. The steward's without a dog right now."

"What does that mean?"

"The steward, the business manager of the place, usually has a hunting dog. He's without a dog right now."

Harry just looked blank.

"He lives down in the row of brick houses," I said. There were about six or eight staff houses, nice brick houses, sitting catty-corner from the administration building and about a block away. They had doctors in them when the hospital could get doctors. If you were a doctor, this wasn't always the best place to work. You could make a whole lot more money somewhere else. The little man was an exception. He liked the work and was willing to stay for less than private-practice doctors made. He had come here to stay for just a little while, and he had ended up staying his whole working career.

"The business manager lives in one of those brick houses," I said. "He doesn't have a dog right now. We could take his doghouse."

"That would be stealing," Harry said.

"That doesn't change the fact, we need a doghouse."

But Harry was stubborn. He made me sneak down and get the doghouse by myself. He said he wouldn't steal it, and I didn't point out that sending me to steal it wasn't much different from stealing it himself.

Have you ever tried to carry a doghouse by yourself? Even just far enough to get it where your sidekick's conscience was assuaged? Harry was perfectly willing to use the doghouse, once I got it out of the man's backyard!

Anyway, once we got the doghouse a decent ways away, we hitched up Pat and Mike to the wagon and took the doghouse out to a little place I often went to get away. It was a small pond out near the hospital cemetery. You got to it by going down a tree-canopied road.

No sooner had we gotten the doghouse in place than Harry said, "I need to go back to the ward and get some blankets."

"Some blankets?"

"It's cold out here," Harry said. "Bullet needs to be kept warm."

Bullet! Harry had named his dog after Roy Rogers' dog, Bullet. Harry had a book I sometimes read to him called *Bullet Leads the Way*. He also saw Bullet on the TV show on the little television in the gathering room. Earlier in the month we had seen the show where the bandits steal Dale's wagon with her baby in it.

So here we were, going back and getting blankets, except now it was Harry's turn to go it alone.

"Get the dog while you're at it," I told Harry.

"He's harder to get out. He don't keep quiet sometimes."

"Well, bring him if you can." And Harry did.

I didn't tell Harry there was something about this place that didn't seem quite right. All the way out, we had other people riding on the wagon with us, evil people who meant harm to us, especially to me.

One of them had told me, just a night or so ago, that the time would come when they would tie me in knots, make me completely ineffective. He had been matter-of-fact about it. "You will be tied in knots and we will be able to do anything we want to with you," he had said. He was the only one who had appeared to me that night.

I found myself talking to him when others weren't watching, almost jabbering. The little man called it a manic episode. But I was good at hiding manic episodes, and I could function despite manic episodes, up to a point. I just couldn't let them come and get me. If they got me, they would do to me what had been done before. They would humiliate me in terrible ways, ways I never shared with anyone.

I was taking my medicine, I thought. And Roy Rogers was protecting me, using his strength and cunning to fend off the bad people, but still they were there.

As Harry and I rode through the tunnel of trees to the little pond, I saw people peering at me, people you would think were just delusions or bad dreams. But they were more than that. I knew that, and I had them with me more of the time than I wanted to admit.

When Harry got back with the little dog, I saw he wasn't a German Shepherd like my Bullet. He was a little Beagle-looking dog, red-blondish with a white patch on his front.

Anyway, we finally got Bullet ensconced in a new doghouse. We tied him to it by a rope. We left him water, but the truth was there was water in the pond. That was a whole lot less likely to freeze than Bullet's water in the bowl.

"We'll bring him scraps to eat," I told Harry as we made our way back to the barn to put the horses up.

"He's used to eating scraps," Harry said. "Roy?"

I looked up.

"Roy. Thanks for caring about Bullet."

I thought he was gonna cry. "That's all I need now," I told Harry. "You crying! Think about it, Harry! You send me to steal the business manager's doghouse. Then we work together to steal the hospital's horses, wagon, blankets, bowls for water, and God knows what else, and we do it all to hide your illegal dog away.

"That's all I need now is to have you crying!"

And then he really cried.

Sometimes Roy Rogers has to go to great lengths to do good things.

"Look, Harry," I said. "We need to get ready for when the little man comes and asks about the doghouse. When they find the doghouse missing, they will suspect us, at least me."

"I won't lie," Harry said.

"You won't need to lie. Just send him to me." Heaven only knows what kind of cock-and-bull story I would give him, but if there was time, I could figure that one out.

"I like the steward," Harry said. "I didn't want to steal his doghouse."

"Neither did I," I told Harry, "but there wasn't any choice. It's wintertime. We needed someplace for Bullet to get in out of the cold."

"Well, if they come and ask me, I won't lie," Harry said again, and believe it or not, they never came. They never asked.

Up until the time I took the doghouse back, I never heard a word about it.

I always thought the steward knew who took the doghouse and why. He probably never even told the little man about it. The steward was a no-nonsense, commonsense sort of person, but he had a big heart too. And he had something else. He had a love of animals. He had grown up farming on a small rural farm. When he got a job for the state, at first it was as a farmhand. But he worked his way up into an important management position.

But he never lost his love of animals. He's one of those people I remember because he kept the horses when they were using tractors and he never came and asked about the doghouse.

# 15

## The Hospital Auditorium

### WEDNESDAY, JANUARY 13, 1954

I don't usually go to hospital dances, but tonight I did. I didn't dance. I just watched the people.

The hospital band, made up of mostly patients, almost always played at patient dances, sometimes with the little man playing on his trumpet. There was a very talented employee who played the piano. She held things together for them all.

The band had a Saturday morning radio show they broadcast from the hospital over a phone line to the local radio station and then to the community as a whole. Also, the band often traveled to Sunrise County community picnics to offer entertainment. It was a way of showing people that the crazies could function. It always gave the little man a chance to say, "Mental illness is an illness just like any other illness." And then he always repeated it, usually several times: "Mental illness is an illness just like any other illness."

For a long time, I didn't understand why he always said that. Then it occurred to me. When this huge place was built, people probably thought us crazy people were possessed by spirits or somehow judged by God. That's why they shuffled us away.

The little man understood things differently. In fact, he understood all of life differently. He knew that people, whether they be mentally ill, physically ill, or different in some other way, were all equal in God's eyes. They were all loved by God. You could do evil things. The little man always talked about things like murder, rape, and exploitation. Those things were wrong. It was wrong to use your mental illness as an excuse to do evil things. He said that a lot to me. He didn't like me beating up on homosexuals, and he wanted me to know it. "You knew what you were doing. You might have sold the authorities a bill of goods. You might have used the demons stalking you as an excuse, but you could have stopped. You could have stopped."

The little man always told me the greatest breakthrough he ever had with me was when I finally admitted I could have stopped. I was doing what I did because I was as mad as hell, but also because I enjoyed it.

"Well, stop enjoying it," he said. "Be Roy Rogers instead. Roy Rogers enjoyed helping people and doing good."

One time I asked the little man, "Why would God make someone crazy?"

"Maybe God's plan just went wrong," he told me. "Maybe the brain got made different in that one little child. Maybe there are chemical imbalances. Or sometimes, maybe we just respond to the terrible things in our own lives. I don't know, Roy. They will know someday, when I'm long gone. But I'll tell you one thing: Even those of us who think we're sane don't know what the future holds."

Years later, I often thought about those words and how they applied to the little man too. But that's for another story at a later time.

As I listened to the hospital band and watched people dance, Harry came over to me. "We need to go see Bullet," he said.

"We can't go at night. Why would we go at night?" I didn't tell him there were nasty demons out there.

He just looked at me with big sad eyes. "We were just there today, Harry," I said. "We took Bullet some food and you had time to play with him."

"He can almost fetch a stick," Harry said proudly.

"And I can almost jump over the administration building too. It doesn't count when you carry the stick to him."

"I love Bullet."

"I know you do. We'll go see him again tomorrow. We can't go more than once a day. If we do, someone will see us. They'll go find Bullet and take him away."

"I wouldn't let them take Bullet away," Harry said, and I just listened. I didn't have the heart to tell him that sometimes bad things happen, no matter what we try to do.

# 16

# At Bullet's House

THURSDAY, JANUARY 14, 1954

People underestimate Harry. They don't just "tend" to underestimate him. They do underestimate him. Harry overhears things he would never overhear if people really understood how much he notices. And he sees things people would not want him seeing.

"George Carson talks to Kurt Harrison," Harry said as we were walking out to take the food to Bullet.

"What?" I asked.

"You told me you found George Carson in the chapel."

"So . . ."

"When we buried that priest man in with Pat, you said you wondered who let the priest man in the record room. Then you said someone told George Carson to come to the meeting in the chapel. I thought about it and thought maybe it was the same person. Maybe all I had to do was watch George Carson."

"They sure wouldn't have paid any attention to you, I suspect."

"I overheard a conversation," Harry said. "Kurt Harrison was asking George Carson if the priest man had showed up. 'I haven't seen him for a while,' Harrision said."

I was floored. "You're sure they were talking about the priest man?"

"I'm sure," Harry said.

He started to say something else when we heard the commotion. We were just entering the tunnel made by the little grove of naked trees. The pond and Bullet were down around the corner, so to speak.

It was as if all hell had broken loose. Bullet's high-pitched yelping filled the air, as did all kinds of other growls and painful sounds.

I looked over at Harry, and I saw a look of panic on his face. He started running. "Something's happening to Bullet," he shouted back at me.

As we came through the trees, we could see a pack of wild dogs. After the initial commotion, they were quietly circling.

In the initial attack, they chewed Bullet badly, but he was still alive. He was partway in his little house, where he had dragged himself.

Harry picked up a large fallen limb. He charged the dogs, and then they turned on him. They tried to circle him, but Harry focused on a huge, long, dark mongrel-looking animal whose ribs were showing. That dog seemed to be the leader.

I never saw Harry so savage, either before or since. He swung the limb so hard the lead dog, as huge as he was, swayed, yelped and drew back. He was obviously hurt. There was no longer so much fire in his deep brown eyes.

The other dogs were circling Harry; one, a smaller black bitch with her teats still hanging, was about to attack him from behind.

By this time, I had gotten my wits about me, and I had my tree limb too. I hit the female dog. I tried to slash at her as savagely as Harry had, but I couldn't do it. I didn't have quite the same feelings Harry did.

Still, the blow distracted the dog and seemed to send the other dogs—most of them were smaller and younger—into even more confusion and retreat. Now they had to fight on two fronts.

The lead dog seemed to evaluate the situation, see that maybe retreat was the better part of valor, and he pulled away. As he did so, the others followed.

By this time, Harry had Bullet in his arms. Bullet was bleeding, but he still seemed to have a lot of life left in him.

"We need to take him to Dr. Jane," Harry said. He was crying now, tears rolling down his bristly, not-recently-shaved cheeks.

"She's a human doctor," I told Harry. She was one of the doctors on the staff.

There weren't very many women doctors anywhere. The fact she was a doctor probably meant she was determined beyond belief. That's the only way women could become doctors back then.

She was probably working at the hospital because people didn't go to women doctors much in 1954.

"She's probably in her office, Harry. We can't go there," I said.

"Yes, we can," he said, cradling Bullet. "I just left him out here to be killed. I just left my dog out here to be killed."

Before I could reply, Harry was gone, in a kind of stumbling run, up through the little tree-tunnel and down the road toward the hospital.

As we left, I saw the meat scraps we had brought flung all over everywhere. Harry had just thrown them to the winds when he heard the dog pack. Now maybe the dog pack could come back to find a little food.

I also saw the delusionary people who were always with me. They were looking out from behind the trees and smiling.

Harry walked straight into the doctor's office. The secretary, the one who kept the patient records and recorded Dr. Jane's notes, was a white-haired lady who had been there forever. She never dressed appropriately for the season. Right now, she was wearing a bright purple, flowered dress.

"You can't go in there!" she said as she stood up and tried to block the way. Harry just pushed her aside, very gently considering the feelings he was having, and walked into the inner office. But Dr. Jane wasn't there.

"Where is she?" I asked the secretary.

"I can't tell you."

"Listen, Marilyn," I told the woman in as reasonable a tone of voice as I could muster, "you may as well tell us, 'cause he's gonna find her, no matter what."

One thing about Marilyn. She was not devoid of common sense. "Dr. Jane's on the women's wards, maybe ward two," Marilyn said. "I'll take you."

So we walked through several of the open wards with people gathering and staring. The women stood around and looked at us. Men never came on the women's wards except for doctors or hospital employees. Male patients weren't supposed to be there, but Marilyn made it so the women didn't scream at our intrusion. Of course, Harry never did anything quietly when he had a full head of steam on.

"I'm not a dog doctor," Dr. Jane told Harry. Her striking, almost purple eyes were troubled. She was a short blondish lady who wore simple dresses, but you could tell, just by looking at her, she was going to help Harry.

"He's just a little dog," Harry said. "He was attacked by a pack of wild dogs."

Harry didn't need to tell her that. She had already decided what she was going to do. "Follow me," she said.

She took us to the little emergency medical office just off the ward, a sort of little surgery where they took care of cuts and bruises and the like.

"Put him here on the table.

"You don't know how much trouble this will cause me," she said with a smile as she examined the dog, even listening to his heart with a stethoscope.

"The little man will understand," I said, and I hoped I was right.

"They tried to rip him apart," she said. "But they didn't get it done. This dog must have some fight in him."

"His name's Bullet," Harry said proudly. "He's a brave dog."

"Like Roy Rogers' Bullet," she said, glancing over at me.

"I didn't give the dog his name," I said.

"I didn't think you did," she answered as she swabbed out Bullet's wound.

"He's really hurt, Harry," she said. "I'm going to sew him up in a couple of places and then take him down to my house. You can stay with him there."

"He will stay alive, won't he?" Harry asked.

"I think so. He's hurt bad, but not bad enough to kill him."

Later that day, a real veterinarian came to Dr. Jane's house to look at Bullet. He was the vet who looked after Pat and Mike and all the cows and mules. I learned later he had dated Dr. Jane for a while. That seemed strange to me. I couldn't visualize anyone dating Dr. Jane.

# 17

## The Steward's Office

### THURSDAY, JANUARY 14, 1954

That afternoon, I just walked into the steward's office. It was different from the doctor's offices. It had more people working there. They were doing financial things.

The steward also did farm things and other kinds of things. He was the one who set up the hunting parties for the packs of dogs.

Being out at the edge of Sunrise, the hospital grounds seemed to be perfect places for townspeople to dump their stray animals, mostly cats and dogs.

The hunting parties killed the cats by finding them when they were having litters and killing the mother and the whole litter. But the dogs roamed more. Mostly they hung around the hospital dump.

Back in 1954 you could have open dumps. In fact, every town did.

Places like the Sunrise Hospital had open dumps too. Our dump had everything in it from old refrigerators to foodstuff. It was acres and acres.

The dogs roamed around the dump because there was food there.

"There's a dangerous pack of dogs," I told the steward when I got to see him. The secretaries didn't want to let me in at first, but I convinced them. "Its leader is a big brownish black dog with a smaller bitch and several pups. The pups look like they're a lot of different ages."

"How do you know about them?" the steward asked.

"Harry saw them hanging around down by the cow herd."

That was a lie, of course, but it would get the steward going. The hospital's milk cow herd was award winning. It had more than one hundred Holstein cows, all of them purebred. It was one of the highest-producing herds in the state. Needless to say, it was the steward's pride and joy. He knew dogs would sometimes corner single cows and, working together, rip them apart.

When I told him that the dogs were down around the cow herd, he perked right up. "We'll take care of it," he said, and I was sure he would.

# 18

## On the Ward

I wasn't surprised when I saw the little man coming across the ward. I even braced myself for what he would probably have to say. But it didn't happen that way.

"You and Harry cause a lot of trouble," he said with a smile.

I just stood there.

"You don't have to tell me where you-all were keeping the little dog. Dr. Jane has said she'll take him now. That way, she'll have a pet. She can get his shots and all, and after a while Harry can go down and visit Bullet—that's his name, right?—any time he wants to."

"She's a nice lady."

"Of course she's a nice lady. She even disinfected the little emergency room herself. Do you know how hard it is to disinfect a place like that?" he added.

I just shook my head.

"Well, she did it herself. She said she didn't think she had the right to ask an employee to do it since she had made the decision to treat a dog there.

"Don't let Harry get another dog," he said. "Be sure Harry knows that Bullet is his dog and Dr. Jane's just keeping Bullet for him. Harry may have to wait awhile to see Bullet. They need to quarantine him," the little man said. "You tell Harry that's just a part of what has to happen."

"I'll be sure to tell him," I said, knowing nothing would keep Harry away from the dog. I wanted to shake the little man's hand and tell him thank you, but no one did that. He might shake your hand once in a while if you had done something especially good, but you didn't shake his. Not that he would have turned you away. It just wouldn't be seemly.

Anyway, before he turned away, the little man said, "I don't know what happened out there, but I'm glad you-all weren't hurt." And then he left.

It wasn't strictly true that we weren't hurt. Later in the day, Harry showed me his leg. It was chewed up and covered with orange stains.

"I didn't tell nobody," Harry said. "I didn't want them trying to treat me instead of Bullet."

"What's the orange stuff, Harry?"

"I took a bottle of that orange medicine they put on wounds," Harry said. "I slipped it in my pocket while Dr. Jane was treating Bullet."

That night, I worried about rabies, but I didn't say anything to Harry or to anyone else. There was no way he would admit he had been bitten, and if I ratted on him, it would be like ratting on your sidekick.

Nowadays, I admit that not telling people Harry had been bitten was probably one of the most stupid decisions I ever made, but we got away with it. The dogs must have been clean of rabies, because Harry and Bullet never got rabies, and that's all that mattered.

# 19

## How to Start a Rumor

### FRIDAY, JANUARY 15, 1954

One way to start a rumor that would shoot around the hospital was to park a police car out in front. This time, there were two, both Sunrise Police cars. When the officers got back from meeting with the little man and then going with him to interview a few patients, they found the car surrounded by a curious crowd.

"Play the siren," someone told the more quiet of the two Sunrise policemen, and the policeman did it.

"They were looking for the man we found there in the record room," Harry told me later. "George Carson said they came to see him and asked if he had seen the priest man."

"Did he tell you who the man was?"

"Just a police officer," Harry said.

"No, not the police officer. The priest man."

"He didn't tell me," Harry said.

"I wonder how they knew the priest man we found had come here to the hospital? He was a stranger to me, and I think I know most everybody, more or less."

"They found some notes or something. He was going to visit a whole lot of people. That's what the notes said. They also found a bunch of old newspapers he had kept for clippings."

"Did the police talk to more people than George?" I asked.

"From what I could tell, they talked to Hoss, to Rosalyn Pope, to Larry over in the lockup, and to a few others. They were especially interested in Larry.

"Larry told me they thought the man was a pervert."

"You talked to Larry?" I asked Harry. No one was allowed on the closed wards. Larry wasn't as good at hiding his demons as I was. He was in and out of the locked ward.

"I have a friend who works that ward. He talked to Larry for me."

"But Larry didn't tell you who the man was, the man they were asking about, I mean."

"Father Coonie," Harry said.

"Harry! Why didn't you tell me that to start with?"

"You didn't ask," he said. Sometimes the relationship between the two of us was like the relationship between Abbott and Costello except even dumber.

"Larry said Father Coonie did some bad things to him and to other people. That was years ago, but some of that had come back up again. He said they were looking for Father Coonie to prefer charges, whatever that is."

I just listened.

"Larry said they had some kind of warrant to talk to the patients. They had contacted their families for permission."

"They would have been working through the little man," I said. "He's known something about all this from the very beginning."

"But he doesn't know about the body," Harry said.

"No," I agreed, "he doesn't know about the body."

Later that night, I heard that Larry had "gone off." He attacked an attendant, and when a group of them tried to subdue him, he bit a nurse on the rear end. He just lifted up her skirt and bit her on the rear end. Obviously, whatever Father Coonie had done to Larry (and I thought I knew what it was), he ruined Larry forever.

In a way, I didn't care much about Larry. I didn't even really know him, but still it made me feel good to know Father Coonie would spend at least the next few years with Pat pooping on him.

# 20

><+><>+O+<>+><

# The Little Store

had to hurry to get to the little store. They usually closed just after five.

"I need another favor," I told Nancy Jane when I got her on the phone. "I need to know about a Father Coonie."

"He was mentioned in the clipping, wasn't he?" she said.

Until she said it, I hadn't thought of it. "He's the one who gave Marcia Weinhart a good recommendation," Nancy Jane added. "Not that it mattered much. She was already dead and whatever her situation was, God didn't need any special recommendations. She already knew."

Nancy Jane was a wonderful lady, but she had a story too. I didn't learn about it until a whole lot later, but when I did learn about it, I understood that, except that she was sane, she was a whole lot like me.

One of the interesting things about Nancy Jane is that I had never heard her refer to God as "he." It was always "she."

Anyway, I told Nancy Jane about the police coming and interviewing people in regard to Father Coonie, and she agreed to find out more about him. I also told her I thought Kurt Harrison was in some way involved with Father Coonie.

"I'll be by on Sunday afternoon," she told me.

# 21

## The Pattern

The weekends were seeming to get into a pattern. I'd call Nancy Jane on Friday. I'd be stymied on Saturday. And then I'd visit with Nancy Jane on Sunday afternoon.

Saturday, I wanted to do something. I wanted to break into Kurt Harrison's locker just to see what was in it. Or failing that, I wanted to confront him and tell him I knew he had been helping Father Coonie find his way around the hospital. The police gave me a way to go at that. In fact, they helped me a lot. Until then, there was no way to tell anybody we had found a body. Now, I could just tell them the police were hunting for a Father Coonie. I could use the police as an excuse to bring him up. Of course, I'd have to come up with some sort of reason to be interested at all, but I could probably do that.

No matter what anyone says, sometimes, the police are helpful.

But I didn't do any of those things. I decided not to break into Kurt Harrison's locker. I didn't want to take the chance of spooking him quite yet. And I couldn't talk to him. He was off on weekends.

Come to think of it, I had seen him around some weekends, probably because he was doing Father Coonie's dirty work, but not this weekend. There wasn't hide nor hair of Kurt this weekend. And so by ten o'clock in the morning I was stymied. Then I got a break. "I have a message from Nevaeh," a male patient on my ward came up and told me. "I seen her out walking the grounds, like always. She says she wants to meet you there."

"Harry says I can trust you," Nevaeh said. "I like to never caught him to ask him about you, what with you-all fooling with that dog all the time."

"Harry loves Bullet," I said.

"He said you love Bullet too. He said you love animals like he does."

"No one loves animals like Harry does."

"I do," she said. "When I was homeless, I used to take homeless animals in. I had a good friend too. I don't know what happened to her. The only thing I don't like about this place is that I had to leave my friend to come here. They don't take niggers here."

"Did you know Father Coonie?" I asked Nevaeh.

"Yeah. He said the children's mass each day."

I must have looked puzzled, because she added, "That's the mass they say for the schoolchildren every weekday morning. We all had to go."

I started to interrupt, but I didn't. She would tell her story in her own good time.

"Father Coonie was using Marcia Weinhart in some way or another," Nevaeh said. "She thought he walked on water. She thought he was a little God. I learned when I was just a little girl you'd better watch out for saints and folks who walk on water."

"Your mother didn't name you, did she?" I asked suddenly.

77

She flinched. "My mother died when I was eight years old. I didn't know my name," she said. "I'm not lyin'. The only name I had until that night my mother froze to death was 'little bitch.'

"My mother used to say, 'You better watch out, you little bitch. I'll kill you.' She was drunk all the time.

"I heard the little man say something wise once. One of the people on the ward was going on about drugs and how terrible they were. The little man overheard it and he said, 'Alcohol abuse is worst of all.'

"I told him he was a smart son of a bitch, and he just smiled and said, 'I'm complimented that you think so.'

"The little man was complimented about something I had told him! I have to tell you, that just made my day."

"So you made up your own name," I said.

"I asked an old man how to spell it. He was my protector back then. In fact, they beat the hell out of him trying to get to me, but he stood up to them and yelled for me to run, and that's what I did. I never knew what happened to him, but I always thought they killed him.

"He was looking after me, not asking any sex for it in return. He was just that kind of man. One day, I told him, 'Marvin, I need a name. I think I'll name myself "Heaven."'

" 'Now little girl,' he said, 'no one's named Heaven.'

" 'Well, I am.'

" 'People will think you're crazy. You can't do that.'

" 'How do you spell "Heaven"?' I asked, and he spelled it for me. 'What about if we spell it backward? It will be like a little code. I'll know what it means, but no one else will.'

" 'How the hell would you say that kind of name?' he asked.

" 'You say it,' I told him. Back then, I didn't know how sounds make words. No one ever taught me.

" 'I guess it's something like *Nev*-ee-ah,' he said, 'with the

78

emphasis on the first syllable.' He was a smart man. He always said he had graduated from college, and I believed him. I don't even know what a syllable is.

"I don't have no use for rich people," Nevaeh said suddenly.

"I think maybe your name's supposed to be Nev-*ay*-ah," I said. "That's what it looks like to me."

"I chose it and I get to say it," Nevaeh said. "Nobody tells me what to do.

"Rich people just ignore you," she added, going back to the original subject. "They pretend that you're not there. Rich people want to live in their little hidey-holes away from all us poor folks. My friend Jacqueline used to say, 'Rich peoples pay you next to nothin' for backbreakin' work. They stab you in the back ever' chance they get. They let you be the ones to fight their wars and all, but most of all, they just don't want to know you're there. They want to go to country clubs where the poor can't go, except for waitresses and maids.'

"I never knew much about country clubs and them things," Nevaeh said. "All I ever knew was that most everybody hates the homeless."

"You're probably right," I said.

"I've been spit on 'cause I'm homeless. That's why this place is so important, Roy. They give you food and a soft bed. People like the little man treat you with respect. That's more than I ever had in my whole homeless life. They throw more food away here every day than I ever had to eat in my whole life, and I don't have to go out in the garbage cans and find it."

"You're right," I said.

"I've only been two places in my life where they really cared—Marcia's and here. If they take this place away, I'll be back at the stockyards. I'll be dead for sure. I won't be strong enough to fend the horny bastards off forever."

"How did you learn Marcia Weinhart had been killed?" I asked.

"She went to church that night and didn't come back. I went and found her. I didn't tell nobody. I just ran away and looked for Jacqueline." Her face melted with grief.

"You were with Marcia Weinhart several years."

"A couple. After my mother died and Marvin was killed, my friend Jacqueline took me in. She was a lot older than me. She was homeless too. We kicked around for several years.

"One time we was run out of the stockyards and we ended up down here.

"Marcia found me and felt sorry for me. She wanted to take me in. I was only twelve years old. Jacqueline said I should go be with Marcia. 'Don't worry about me,' Jacqueline said. 'You'll be better off with her. She has a house and all.' In some ways, leaving Jacqueline was the hardest thing I ever did, but she was right. I was better off.

"Marcia Weinhart made me go to Catholic school. That's where I learned to read. The nuns worked with me special. They said I was smart.

"Marcia sent me to the dentist and the doctor. She told me she would make a lady out of me.

"When George Carson told me about Marcia, he didn't know I already knew her. I knew Father Coonie too.

"George was bitching about Marcia Weinhart, saying what a piece of crap she was. He said she set young boys up. Then I told him he was wrong. I told him she took me in.

"'She let that old priest rape me and the others,' George Carson told me. I didn't believe it, but I didn't tell him that again."

Later that day, Nevaeh came back to see me. "There's something I don't think you understand," she said. "The rich people

80

hate this place. They want it closed. It's not uptown enough for them."

I didn't know what to say. She was right of course. In Sunrise, people like Nancy Jane were the exception. A lot of the people in Sunrise hated this place because they thought it made the town inferior. Even some of the employees hated it.

"They'll get it closed one day," Nevaeh said. "I promise you they will. And when they do, I'll be back out under bridges, except I'll be raped this time. I'll have some great big stud pull down my panties and stick himself in me or even kill me, and I'll be so sick and tired I can't stop it."

"Maybe the hospital won't close," I said.

"It will close," she said. "It's not a perfect place. It's got all kinds of things wrong with it until you have to live under bridges and be raped instead. Some people like that life even better, but I don't. I like it here. They feed me and they have soft beds. I don't have to have sex with nobody. I'm safe here."

"Why did Father Coonie want to see you?" I asked Nevaeh.

"I don't know. Father Hogan was the one who told me Coonie was going to look me up. He said he wasn't helping Coonie. He didn't think Coonie should come to see folks like me, but still, Father Hogan wanted me to be warned. Father Hogan liked me." Father Lucian Hogan was the hospital chaplain.

"Did Father Hogan let Coonie in the record room?"

"Nah. He did everything he could to keep Coonie away from this place. He said Coonie was all mixed up, demented now. He seemed to like Coonie, but he didn't want Coonie around here.

"Father Hogan's a nice man, Roy. He tries to help you when you need it. I don't go to his church or nothin'. I don't believe in churches. If there was a God like all these churches tell you, then why do people like me get raped under bridges? And why do the rich people always win?"

"But you're named Heaven," I said.

"Heaven's what I want that I can never have," Nevaeh said. "The only heaven is right here in this place, and when the rich people stomp it in the ground the way they will—you just watch; they will—when they stomp it in the ground, I'll be dead too."

"Carpe diem," I replied.

"What the hell is that?"

"Some sort of language that means 'seize the day.' Make the best of what you've got today. Whether they kill this place or not, you've got this place today. Make the best of it."

"You sound like Father Hogan," Nevaeh said.

## 22

# On the Bench in Front of the Willow

## SUNDAY, JANUARY 17, 1954

Y ou really have a nose for nastiness," Nancy Jane told me when she met me on Sunday afternoon. "Father Coonie was accused of raping altar boys. I didn't know anything about it. It happened when I was just a little girl," she said.

"The story wasn't in the newspaper," she said. "Thank God for *The Sentinel*'s white-headed editor. His name is Red. He is a Catholic himself. He says Coonie was caught in the act of raping a little boy in the vestry behind the altar. He had raped a lot of them in a lot of places over the years.

" 'The diocese got involved and covered the whole thing up,' the editor told me. 'It was never in the paper, and it never went much beyond a few people in the church.'

"That's what they did back then," she said. "It's what they still do. They cover up and then send the priest on to some other unsuspecting parish."

"We live in a world filled with justice and good action," I replied in my most holier-than-thou tone, and she just smiled.

"Anyway, the editor was ticked off, but there wasn't much he could do. He wasn't the editor back then. He was just a cub reporter. He wanted to do an investigative story, but he had made a mistake and his job was on the line.

"It was the policy back then to report people's illnesses when they went into the hospital. They would just put it in the paper: 'Nancy Jane Garber Enters Hospital for Female Problems,' and then they would write all the gory details.

"Of course it wasn't quite that bad," she said, "but almost."

I just listened.

"There was a suicide attempt, a lady from a wealthy family. The young cub reporter put it in there just as it happened, how she had been rushed to the hospital following a suicide attempt with all the details. He almost lost his job. The publisher was incensed. 'You don't write stories like that about the such-and-such family!' he screamed at the young man. And when the young man asked why not since the newspaper would expect its reporters to write them about other people, the publisher just said, 'This is different. This is different.'

"So the young man passed the Coonie story up."

"It's an interesting world, isn't it?" I said. Very few things made my stomach churn, but this thing did.

"I made a deal with him, Roy."

"The editor?"

"Actually, it wasn't a deal exactly. I did a quid pro quo."

"You told him about the police interviewing people out here about Father Coonie." My heart sank.

"No. I didn't think that would be fair. You're trying to break your neck not to involve the hospital in this. I didn't think I should either. I just told him to check with the police. They were once again looking into Father Coonie.

"After all, he's helped us, Roy. He's helped us a lot."

"They won't tell him exactly what they're doing," I said. "At least I hope they won't."

"If I thought they would have, I wouldn't have given him Father Coonie's name, but if they know he has inquired, they might call him first when it comes time to charge Coonie."

All of a sudden, Nancy Jane was shivering. "It's cold out here," she said. "Let's go in and play some dominoes, and this time you're not supposed to let me win, even one little game."

I didn't.

It wasn't until after she left that I thought of something else I wanted to ask Nancy Jane.


Later that night, I asked myself why I was messing with this at all. Why did I care who killed Father Coonie? And why did I care who killed Marcia Weinhart a whole bunch of years ago?

But then I thought of Roy Rogers. Roy Rogers wouldn't let a thing like this go. He would see it through to the end. He would see the culprits brought to justice, and so should I.

If I did it the other way, I'd be like the newspaper was. They only report the bad news, the suicides and the like, of poor people. The rich people get off scot-free.

In Roy Rogers' world, no bad guy got off scot-free, no matter who he was or how much power and money he had.

As I went to sleep that night, I knew that the only way to keep my stomach from churning was for me to live in Roy Rogers' world.

# 23

⊳─┼─◆⟩──◯──⟨◆─┼─⊲

# About the Switchboard

**MONDAY, JANUARY 18, 1954**

I had to wait until Monday to call Nancy Jane again.

With my access, you would have thought I could have just sneaked into someone's office and placed a call, but I couldn't. All the phone calls went through a central switchboard, one of those old kind with the operator who plugged you in.

Years later when I saw that lady who did the thing with, "One ringy dingy, two ringy dingies," I thought about the switchboard.

Anyway, they kept the switchboard open all night long. In fact, there were an amazing number of phone calls back and forth between wards and from the wards to doctors. That was back at a time when doctors really took night calls.

Any call placed from any office would have been identified as coming from that office and would have to go through the operator.

There was one thing about sneaking down into the big marble-floored lobby. The enclosed office with the switchboard was at the front of the lobby. The switchboard office didn't command a view of the stairs, so you could sneak down the stairs and around by the Double Cola machine without being noticed, but if you went too far into the lobby, they would see you.

In other words, I had to wait until Monday morning to call Nancy Jane.

When I got her, I said, "Can you find out the connection between Father Coonie and Marcia Weinhart?" I already thought I knew what it was, but still I needed confirmation. "See if there was anything more than that he was just her priest."

That night Nancy Jane came by for just a minute. "Marcia Weinhart was the one who made the altar schedule," Nancy Jane said. "She was a friend of a Catholic friend of my family named Adrienne Powell. That's how I found out."

"In other words, Marcia Weinhart decided who would be the altar boys," I said.

"You've got it," Nancy Jane replied. She started to say something else, but then she didn't.

So it was just the way I thought! Marcia Weinhart covered for Coonie, making it so that Coonie himself didn't have to schedule particular altar boys at early masses. He could just ask her to do it. (I was sure it was early masses, probably 6:00 or 7:00 A.M. Back in the 1950s Catholic churches always had early masses and hardly anyone attended or stayed to talk to the priest afterward.)

Coonie was a conniving son of a bitch! He knew what he was doing.

That's one thing the little man taught me. Some people rape, commit sexual acts of violence, on the spur of the moment, but serial rapists plan what they are going to do. They connive because they have to. Regular homosexuals are just ordinary people with a different private inclination.

A person's sexual inclination (that's what the little man called it) was not the issue. The issue was force and violence, and the issue with serial rapists was *planned* force and violence. "Attacking homosexuals doesn't do anything to stop rape," the little man told me over and over again.

If I had been talking to the little man about Father Coonie, he would have said, "It wouldn't be any different than if the priest molested young girls in a planned way. In fact, I'm sure some do. The issue is rape, not homosexuality. The issue is violent exploitation."

The little man was insistent. "Homosexual people or non-homosexual people are just people," he told me once. "Only when they abuse children or use force to get what they want from children or adults should they be treated differently and punished."

Of course, he talked to me so much about all these things because of why I was here. I and a bunch of teenaged friends attacked a homosexual. We beat the hell out of him in much the same way some people attack and beat homeless people, even today. I was smart enough they never really proved it, but my record still has stark black-and-white pictures of a couple people lying on the ground in their own blood, their faces caved in where we had kicked them and tried to kill them. The cops turned those over just so the little man would know what an SOB I really was. They didn't like it when I ended up in Sunrise.

"You can't always prove the truth," the police told the little man after they brought me in. They even made a special effort to come and talk to him in hopes he'd make it harder for me.

But the truth was I didn't really want to kill those people. I wanted them to suffer. Back then, making other people suffer, especially queers, made me feel good.

Sometimes I thought about stealing the pictures in the record and destroying them, but that would be tantamount to confessing I rummaged through the records, so I couldn't do it. I had to leave things be, especially obvious things in my own record.

"It's not right to want anyone to suffer," the little man told me once as he kept at me about all this. "Rapists make people suffer, and violent teenagers or adults make folks suffer too."

All this seems so obvious now that we're so far from the 1950s, but that was a different time. People had different attitudes about Negroes and homosexuals. Some (including some so-called Christians) still do.

The little man didn't fool me. He was doing what I would call informal psychotherapy. He didn't do it in an office or in some structured way. He just talked to you about what your issue was. He talked to you, and he tried to be sure you got your medicine.

"You're a smart man, Roy," the little man told me. "You already knew you were in the wrong. You were changing before I even knew you. You had already chosen another way, a different model, Roy Rogers. You can use your brain to change your behavior. Not everybody's like that."

"I didn't use my brain," I told him skeptically. "Stop and think about it. Folks like Roy Rogers and Gene Autry and Hopalong Cassidy molded and changed a whole generation. I just came to Roy Rogers later than most kids did."

"You just pretend you're Roy Rogers," the little man said.

"Even Roy Rogers wasn't Roy Rogers," I told the little man. "He started with another name. And before he was called Trigger, Trigger was named Golden Cloud."

The little man just smiled.

*If you're reading this manuscript, you are a much younger member of my family who doesn't have any idea what it was like to grow up in the thirties, forties, and fifties. Because that's true, I think there's something I need to tell you. Back then, Roy Rogers was more than just a hero. He was a man who changed people's lives, sometimes even terrible people like me.*

# 24

## On the Ward

After I went through Kurt Harrison's locker, I left him a note telling him I needed to talk to him.

He came late at night. He worked the three-to-eleven shift, but this was much later.

"I dare you to go through my locker!" he whispered hoarsely as he shook me awake.

"I already have," I said. I was still foggy, but I could see the fire in his eyes.

"And you'll be reported!" He had pulled me to my feet. He was a compact man, maybe five feet eight or so. He had dark curly hair and usually hooded eyes. He looked much younger than he probably was.

"You won't report me, and you know it," I said. "The police were here asking about Father Coonie. When you report me and they take me in, I'll just tell them I suspect you of being the one who let Father Coonie into the hospital and showed him the way around. In fact, I'll go even further than that. I'll show them the passkey I found in your locker, the passkey you used to let

Coonie go wherever he wanted. No one but the little man and the business manager should have a passkey. That key will open any door on the place."

I was talking quietly, but I could hear some movement down the ward. Harrison must have heard it too. We both froze like startled rabbits. "We need to talk," Harrison said when the noise settled. "We need to go someplace private." And that's what we did.

# 25

## The Park

The private place ended up being the public park the next day. I didn't want to talk to Harrison that night. For one thing, it would be hard to find a place where we could talk privately, and for another, I didn't want him to choose the time and place. I wanted to meet him on what a different generation would later call my "turf."

My initial reaction was to want to get the whole thing over, so I thought about talking in one of the bathrooms, but that was too risky. The wards were long halls lined with two-person rooms. Each room had two rocking chairs outside of it. Those chairs went clear back to the time people assumed lunatics could be happy spending their days sitting and rocking outside their rooms.

But that was beginning to change in 1954. By then, they had discovered the first tranquilizers. Believe it or not, before that, some people believed lunacy was an inherited character defect, as if being crazy was your own fault. Those folks had said things like, "Lock the crazies up to keep them from breeding," and that's what they did. Even in the 1950s a few were still talking about sterilization and lobotomies as treatments for mental illness.

But now, because of a few medicines, there were more patients who were calm enough to be allowed freedoms. These patients were often up and down at night and often in the communal restrooms. The restrooms wouldn't be a good place to go to talk.

"Let's meet tomorrow," I said. "Let's go down to the park."

At first Harrison wanted to protest, but then he gave in, actually without much fuss. That was my first clue that I had him over a barrel, to put it in a gentle way.

The park sat in line with the main building, about half a mile or so down a road that ran westward from the edge of the central campus. The road ran between the staff houses and some lesser buildings.

On your way, you went by another pond—the grounds were filled with ponds—and before that by a small grape arbor (yes, the hospital farm did raise grapes!) and by the chicken farm. Then you came to the park.

The park was there from the beginning of the lunatic asylum. It was dedicated to the memory of some famous man. I don't know whether he gave the land or what.

"You can't show them the key," Kurt Harrison said as soon as I was within speaking distance. "If you did, you'd have to tell them you'd been in my locker."

"If you turn me in, they'll know that anyway. Besides, I can tell them I think you're the one who let Father Coonie in. I can tell them I saw you with him."

"That's a lie! They won't believe you."

"They'll investigate. The little man knows I don't tell him lies. They'll investigate."

That seemed to set Harrison back.

Just to make the sale, I added, "They'll talk to the other ones involved in all of this, maybe even to the other employees or friends you told about it, and they'll find out. I guarantee it."

"Well, it's over now," Harrison said. "At least it seems to be. What will you gain by ratting on me? Do you want money? Is that it? You want money!"

"Listen, Kurt . . . ," I said. It felt good to call him Kurt. "Listen, Kurt, I'm the one who asks the questions here," and that was my mistake. I lorded it over him, and suddenly he changed.

"Put your cards on the table," he said coldly.

I must have seemed confused.

"Put your cards on the table, or I walk away." He was a whole different man.

"You knew Coonie when he was in Sunrise," I replied, just guessing but fairly sure. "You had some kind of relationship with Coonie. You were showing him around because he was your friend or because he had something on you."

Kurt Harrison just laughed. "Research it, friend," he said with anger in his voice. "I didn't even come to Sunrise until after Coonie left. You're so smart. Go to the record room and look it up, or have your friend ask around the town!"

My neck hairs bristled. He knew about Nancy Jane. He was good at watching too. "I didn't have any connection with Father Coonie," he said.

"Then how did you come to know him?"

"I didn't know him. That's the point. And you'll play hell proving I did."

After that, I expected him to say something else, but he didn't. I expected him to say, "You'll be sorry for this. You will pay."

Instead, he just turned—we were close to park tables and benches, but neither of us had ever sat down—and then walked away.

## 26

❦❧

# Visiting Bullet

**WEDNESDAY, JANUARY 20, 1954**

The next day, Harry was confined to the ward.

I received a note written by some friend of Harry's. Harry couldn't write, except his name. "Confined to ward," it said. "Go see Bullet for me. Harry."

Instead, I went to see the little man. "Harry's been confined to the ward," I said.

"Supposedly there's been some difficulty," the little man replied. "I've arranged for an immediate staffing. That's all I can say."

I didn't try to push him any further. For one thing, you couldn't push the little man. So I did go to see Bullet.

Bullet had a new doghouse now. Dr. Jane must have gone into town to buy it. Bullet was kept outside chained to the doghouse during the day when Dr. Jane was at work, but then at night she let him in her own house. In a way, Bullet had the best of both worlds. Also, Dr. Jane had taken to letting Harry come by her house and get Bullet, put a leash on him, and walk him through the park. She said the exercise was good for the very quickly recovering dog. It kept him from getting stiff, she said.

Harry had already walked Bullet a time or two. Today I walked Bullet for Harry.

# 27

## The Record Room

That night, I went to the record room. There in Harry's file was the complaint. Kurt Harrison had written Harry up, saying he was becoming violent. "Patient refused to go to his room and then spit on the employee," Harrison had written.

> *Growing signs of mental disturbance [the note continued]. Making paper flowers in recreational therapy and putting them on graves out at the patients' cemetery, stealing flowers and placing them in a horse stall, hiding an unallowed animal under bed and refusing to move it when told. Direct contradiction of the attendant's orders.*
>
> *Recommendation: immediate confinement to the ward with possibility of further confinement and other treatment.*

"Other treatment" meant electric shock. Harrison was hinting Harry needed electroshock treatment, something almost every patient dreaded, even though it sometimes helped.

*Resolution: [the form went on] Patient immediately staffed. Medication increased. Ward confinement and observation to be continued three days, including day confined.*

"Including day confined." That meant the little man was on Harry's side. The very fact that the staffing was in the record that same day probably spoke well for Harry. The little man had probably brought it down and put it there himself. He didn't usually do that. This time, he didn't want it lost in the flow of paper.

But Harry wouldn't let it be. Wednesday night early, just after dark, Harry sneaked out of the ward, went down to Dr. Jane's house, put Bullet on his leash, and went to hide out.

Unfortunately, Dr. Jane was working late that night and hadn't yet taken Bullet in. Dr. Jane often worked late.

Later Harry would tell me, "I wasn't going to let them keep me on the ward. I didn't do anything. I didn't even see Harrison last night when he said I spit on him."

"He's getting back at *me*, Harry," I said.

"Well then, let him do something to you."

But Harrison didn't want to draw attention to me. Somehow he knew he was safe because I couldn't afford to have the spotlight put on Father Coonie. Harrison also knew that to hurt Harry was probably a better way to hurt me than to hurt me would be.

So Harry escaped from the ward, stole Bullet, and then went down and tried to hide in Pat's horse stall.

Unfortunately, Bullet had never been around horses. He panicked, and even though he was still bandaged up and stiff, he started yelping and biting at Pat's heels. Needless to say, Pat didn't like that, kicked at Bullet, and kicked out the back of the stall. Then before Harry could do anything, Pat's co-horse, Mike, became upset and started kicking in his stall too.

The only thing that saved us was that there was no one around right then. Harry had sense enough to pull Bullet out of the stall. It was probably a miracle Harry himself or Bullet weren't kicked in the head by the horse. If Harry had been kicked, someone would have found him and then they would have probably found Father Coonie's grave. After that, all hell would have broken loose for sure.

But fortunately for all of us, it didn't happen that way. Instead, Harry grabbed Bullet up, took him back to Dr. Jane's, and then, very early Thursday morning, sneaked into the hospital to get me. We got the damage repaired, at least enough, and we got Harry back to the ward just before daylight.

"Use your head, Harry," I told him as we were walking back. "When they caught you, they'd have put you on a closed ward almost forever."

"Nah," Harry said, "not the little man. He wouldn't do that."

So all's well that ends well, you might say, except it didn't happen that way. By this time, they had missed Harry. They thought they were trying to keep a close eye on him, but they really weren't.

The full alarm had gone out. The sheriff was out looking in the county, and the little man, the business manager, and a whole lot of others were scouring the cemetery across the road and the other places where escapees went to hide. The little man always went out and looked for people. The steward/business manager sometimes did, though he never thought it was as important as the little man did.

Meanwhile, Harry and I were back on the ward, but of course they knew Harry had escaped.

"We're probably in real trouble now," I told Harry when it was clear exactly what was happening.

"Pat wouldn't hurt me," Harry said. "I love animals. Pat

wouldn't hurt me." He always had a way of sending conversations careening off in some other direction.

"No," I said, "but Kurt Harrison would. Kurt Harrison would hurt us both."

"You guys make it hard for me to help you," the little man told me when I saw him later. "You tell Harry to keep his butt on the ward until we let him off. It will probably be another week now." I told Harry.

# 28

# The Record Room

THURSDAY, JANUARY 21, 1954

Sometimes when you hit a brick wall, the thing to do is rummage.

I did my rummaging in the record room. I rummaged through Kurt Harrison's file, and it was like he said. He hadn't come to Sunrise until the late 1940s, long after Coonie had come and gone.

There was no indication in the file that Harrison had ever known Coonie.

But while I was in the employee files, I decided to look up the hospital chaplain Father Hogan too. I wondered if maybe he had some connection to Father Coonie. Maybe Hogan had been raised in Sunrise or served as an assistant pastor in Sunrise some time or other.

But that wasn't the case. Hogan was born and raised in a town clear across the state. He attended seminary at an abbey in a place I had always considered a vacation Mecca. Insofar as I could tell, they had never served together in a parish.

Father Hogan was a chaplain, a middle-aged man who worked

in places exactly like the insane asylum where he was right now. He was supposedly trained for that, whatever that meant way back then.

In so far as I could tell, he and Father Coonie never crossed paths.

As I closed Father Hogan's record, I thought of what I knew of him. I only talked to Father Hogan extensively one time. It was after church. I hung around the chapel waiting for him. I wanted to ask him to see if he could get Harry out of lockup.

Harry had hidden some feral cats.

Harry hated to see the cats killed. They killed the cats by incinerating them in the super-hot firebox at the electric plant. They tried to find the litters before they had even opened their eyes. Then they destroyed the cats.

It was almost necessary. People dropped cats and dogs off out at the hospital by the boatload. There was no way to find homes for all of them. If you let them run, you ran the risk of rabies and other kinds of things. Cats were especially bad. They had large litters, reproduced before they were a year old, and became truly wild.

In later years, I read somewhere that there is no way to tame a truly feral cat.

Anyway, Harry tried to save a litter. He had seen the farm people he worked with carry off the cats and kill them. He decided to do something about it.

"How were you gonna feed 'em, Harry?" I asked him later.

"I had a little doll milk bottle," Harry said. He was serious. He even offered to show it to me.

"And you didn't think they'd catch you?"

"It don't matter, Roy. They shouldn't kill those little cats."

"You're right. They shouldn't," I said. "The people who leave them shouldn't leave them either."

So I waited as Father Hogan took off his vestments, came out and fiddled around in the tabernacle, arranging things exactly the way they were supposed to be inside, and then turned to leave.

I explained to Father Hogan what Harry had done and why he was in lockup. "This time the little man is sorta mad," I said. "He won't help Harry this time."

And Father Hogan laughed. Then he got serious and said, "Lockup's not a punishment. It's a treatment. It's a failure if you have to be in there forever. And it's a failure if you use it like they're using it right now."

I just nodded.

"I've had people help me, Roy. I've had people change my life," he said. "I had a teacher once who made all the difference in the world to me. I'll do what I can."

And he did. By the next day, Harry was out of the lockup ward and back where he should be.

"Don't go trying to save cats again," I told Harry.

"I can't help it, Roy." He was crying, truly crying. "They didn't even have their eyes open yet."

So I went to the farm manager, the underling to the steward. I explained to him how Harry felt about the cats.

"There's not much else to do," the man said dismissively.

"How about just being quieter about it? Harry works around this place. Don't do it where he knows about it. Keep what's happening from Harry."

That's what they did. It took awhile for Harry to forget, but in a little while Harry started trying to save dogs instead.

Later, Harry told me, "Father Hogan is my friend now. He got me out. He even reads to me from his book of poetry."

"His book of poetry?"

"He writes poems. About sunsets and rolling rivers and motherhood and things like that. He says he keeps his book here at the hospital so he can write in it at work. I go visit him, and if he has it with him, he reads what he calls his 'latest poem.' It's fun."

To each his own, I guess. The last thing in the world I would have said of my friend Harry was, "He enjoys poetry."

Both the records and my own knowledge about Father Hogan didn't lead me to suspect him at all.

Things were different with the records way back then. Nowadays, you would put them on a computer and do a search. I know about things like that. I like records. In later years, when I was over eighty-five, I learned computers and especially databases. My instructor said I was a genius at it. But there weren't any computers or databases back then. They tried to index the records in various ways, mostly by keeping lists of what you might call cross-references. One of those cross-references was to Sunrise.

That cross-reference showed that the only present people in the institution with traceable Sunrise history were people like Rosalyn Pope, George Carson, and Larry over in the lockup. If there were other connections, they would have to be among employees, and how could someone like me deal with that? I surely couldn't go around and ask employees, "Did you know Father Coonie?" And I couldn't suggest that someone else do it either, since I couldn't afford to be directly connected to the priest.

I was still facing a brick wall.

# 29

## Kurt Harrison

### THURSDAY, JANUARY 21, 1954

That night, Kurt Harrison was beaten. It didn't happen at the hospital. It happened at his apartment.

Harrison was a divorced man who lived alone. His daughter found him lying in a pool of blood. She called the police, but Harrison told the police he didn't know who did it. His daughter was convinced he knew, but still, Harrison refused to say anything about it.

Whoever beat him had laid in wait for Harrison. They knew he worked the three-to-eleven shift, and they were waiting for him when he came home.

They seemed to want to know something, probably the whereabouts of Father Coonie, but Harrison didn't tell them. He couldn't tell them, but they didn't know that.

After spending some time in the emergency room, Harrison went back home, locked his doors, and tried to rest so he could go to work again tomorrow.

I found out all this from Nancy Jane. She said the white-haired editor at *The Sentinel* had told her. A reporter had heard the ambulance call and, knowing it involved violence, followed up.

The next day, Friday, Nancy Jane made a special trip out to the hospital to tell me what had happened. I had just gotten done arguing with the little man, so I might not have been as cordial as I should have been, but when she told me, I apologized. "I'm sorry to be so short with you," I said. "I've been arguing with the little man about clothes."

"Arguing about clothes?"

"He says we shouldn't wear overalls."

"You always wear overalls. You've worn them ever since I knew you."

"We get our clothing from a commissary," I said. "That way, we get to pick them ourselves.

"Anyway, the little man has got it in his head overalls aren't dignified. He says we should wear shirts and slacks. He outlawed overalls from the choices except for people like Hoss who need them for his work."

"What does he care one way or the other?" Nancy Jane asked.

"Well, you know the little man. He can be a stubborn SOB when he gets some crazy idea in his head. He's always saying, 'Mental illness is an illness just like any other illness.'

"He thinks he's educating people, telling them that they were wrong when they built this place."

"Wrong?" Nancy Jane said. She smiled a little, and I knew that sometimes I amused her. She enjoyed egging me on.

"They built this place in the late eighteen hundreds to keep the crazies out of the general population. Back then, people saw crazy people as having character disorders. When God made them, creation somehow misfired.

"There was nothing wrong with throwing crazy people away, putting them someplace like this. They were inferiors to begin with. Incarceration just made common sense."

"People still feel that way," Nancy Jane said. "At least a lot of them do. They just don't say it."

I only nodded.

"But what's that got to do with how you dress?" She was smiling now, trying to keep me going.

"He wants us to be walking billboards. Like I said, he's always saying, 'Mental illness is just another illness like any other illness.' He wants us to look like what he thinks is normal. He wants us to look like anyone else who's sick, and he's gotten it into his head that we can do that better if we dress in shirts and slacks."

"So?"

"So the first thing I did," I told her, now smiling too, "was break into the commissary to steal a bunch of overalls and hide them so I'd have some in reserve. Then I argued with him."

"Who won?" she asked, almost laughing now.

"You don't win with the little man. He's too stubborn. But he is honest too. He'll think about what I said, and finally, he'll change his mind. He'll know I was right."

"He's a good man, isn't he?" Nancy Jane said.

"The best," I said, "but I wouldn't tell him that. He might get the big head."

# 30

## The Icehouse

Friday morning I received a note from Larry in the lockup. "Meet me at the icehouse—10:30 tonight," the note said.

"How can Larry meet me there? He's in the lockup," I told the friend who brought the note.

"Larry has his ways," my friend said. "He's not as helpless as they think he is."

The icehouse was kind of an anachronism. Years before it had been of great use. Before the wide use of Freon in refrigeration, the institution used iceboxes to keep things cold. You took a fifty-pound block of ice or whatever, and you put it in the bottom of the icebox.

Iceboxes and large coolers full of ice were what everyone used back then. At first, icehouses were built near lakes. When the lakes froze, they cut out chunks of ice and stored them in the insulated buildings, even through the summer. Later, I suppose they used electricity to somehow make the ice. I don't think I ever really knew for sure.

When I was a little boy, I used to go to my grandmother's in a small rural town. I loved to go there. It was an escape for me. My childhood at home wasn't happy. I would sit out on her front porch and watch as the people across the street put printed signs in their windows. They were white cardboard signs with black numbers on them. A sign would say something like "50," or whatever. When the horse-drawn ice wagon came, the iceman delivered that amount of ice. He took his x-like tongs, hooked into a fifty-pound block of ice, and lugged it to the house.

Later, they used trucks to make the deliveries. And even later, they just switched to electric refrigerators, so the icehouses died.

But the icehouse was still working at the hospital. It still made limited amounts of ice, in the same blocks as always, probably for chipping up and cooling drinks and the like.

The icehouse was right next to the power plant, close to the electricity, I suppose. It was probably moved some time after the power plant was built. Also, someone told me the power plant and the icehouse used some of the same chemicals, so they were built close together.

Anyway, it was always freezing in the icehouse with its stark white walls and translucent blocks of ice.

Larry was wearing a short-sleeved shirt, but he didn't seem cold at all. I was all bundled up.

Larry was tormented. He faced, almost all the time, what I faced intermittently. I didn't know his demons. Even when you have your own, you can't claim to know someone else's, but I did know how paralyzing such things could be.

"Kurt Harrison is the one who gave Coonie access to the hospital," Larry told me. He seemed to know a lot about what I had been doing.

"I figured that," I said.

"Coonie paid him. He paid a lot."

"Paid him for access to the hospital?"

"One thousand dollars every time."

I was flabbergasted. "Where did Coonie get a thousand dollars?"

"Coonie was a rich man," Larry said. "His mother was rich. One way she protected him is that she gave tens of thousands of dollars to the church. The people in the diocese knew which side their bread was buttered on."

"Is Coonie's mother still alive?" I asked.

"She's been dead a long time now."

"And you knew Coonie from when you were a child?"

Larry stood rock still and even his green eyes got harder. "I knew Coonie from when I was an altar boy in the church," he said.

"Who beat up Kurt Harrison?" I asked.

"I don't know that," Larry said.

"How did Kurt Harrison get to know Father Coonie?" I asked. That was really the operative question now.

"I don't know," Larry said. "I just know Coonie paid him to be shown around. I wouldn't be surprised if Harrison killed Coonie."

I kept my mouth shut. Larry was an amazing man, ice-cold on the inside, maybe capable of killing in his own right, and yet he seemed to know a lot about what was happening around the hospital. When he was normal (which wasn't very often), he seemed to be just like everybody else, so much so that he sometimes had ground privileges like I did. Other times, they locked him up. He gave them behavior clues when he was about to go off.

"Harry told me you-all found Coonie dead," Larry said. "He wouldn't tell me where you buried Coonie. He said that was a 'confidential' matter."

I had to smile. Harry was such a literal person. He knew he wasn't supposed to tell *anybody* where Father Coonie had been buried. He just didn't think that applied to telling people Coonie had been killed.

"I hope Harry hasn't been going around telling everybody about Father Coonie's death."

"Nah. I talked to him about that," Larry said. "I told him he should keep his big lips buttoned."

I just nodded.

"I admire Harry," Larry said. "He told me that when he was a boy, he lived next to a neighbor who tortured animals. Harry saw the neighbor do it one time. He ran crying home, and his mother told him not to ever tell anybody what he saw.

"The man who tortured animals ended up torturing and killing people too, but Harry went another way," Larry said.

"His heart was softened," I replied.

"I always wish it would have happened that way with me," Larry said, "but I was different."

"It was you being tortured."

He nodded curtly. "They're talking about letting me out of lockup a few hours a day."

"It'll never happen if they catch you out right now."

"They won't catch me," Larry said.

As Larry turned to leave, I found myself wondering why he could sometimes be allowed to roam. Then I remembered what the little man had told me once. There is an ethics to this being crazy. You can be crazy, but you can't use your crazy to be bad.

When I thought about it later, I suspected that's how it was with Larry. He wasn't the kind of man to hide his bad with crazy. When he was crazy he was dangerous and he needed to be locked up, but when he wasn't, he wasn't bad either. He was just another patient in the Sunrise asylum. Maybe the medicines were giving him fewer crazy days, or maybe he'd just somehow decided to have fewer now that he was helping Harry.

Just before he left, Larry turned back to me and said, "If I can help the little man, I want to do it. I owe the little man."

"Oh?"

"I have these episodes, these times when I go berserk. Really, it's more than that. I don't even know what I'm doing. I attacked a person one time. He ended up being hurt pretty bad, and they put me in jail in another county, one away from here.

"Those folks in there weren't just crazy, Roy. They were bad. They wanted me to do things I couldn't do, things I'd promised myself I'd never do again, and when I wouldn't do those things, they beat me almost to death. I didn't fight them. I should have, but I was just hard-assed stubborn. I decided this time I wasn't going to fight back. I was in that city's hospital for almost a month. Sometimes you can't just go off on cue. If I had gone off, those folks who beat me would have been toast. But it didn't happen that way. They weren't dealing with crazy Larry."

I didn't say anything.

"Well, the sheriff was a good ol' boy in his own way. When it was time for me to get out of the hospital and go back to jail, he called the little man and asked to transfer me here to the Sunrise State Hospital. It took a lot of doing. They had to go before a court and all. It was going to complicate things because I came from Sunrise and they had tried to run me out of Sunrise, get me as far away from here as possible. There was every reason not to allow the transfer.

"Just before I left to come here, the sheriff called me in and said, 'He's doing you a favor down there. He didn't have to do this, but he said you deserved the chance. Don't mess it up.'

"I owe the little man. He took a chance on me. He probably

saved my life. I wouldn't have survived in that place, not in the long run."

"It all had to do with what happened to you and Father Coonie."

"I had mental trouble before that. I was born with it, my parents said. They were already having me go to doctors. But I snapped with Coonie. I wasn't near as big as he was—I was just an ordinary-sized kid—but I tried to climb his legs, so to speak, get up in his face, and scratch his eyes out.

"That's the first time I ever heard an actual snap in my mind, like a strong dry branch breaking. I attacked Father Coonie. That's when they started looking into all this seriously. No one really knew why I had done it.

"It was years later when I attacked the man and almost killed him. I snapped that time too.

"Once in a while, I still hear that quick, sharp snap. I can't keep it from happening. And when it's over, I don't know what I've done to people. But I do my best to keep the snap away. I do better now than I used to. They give me medicine. The little man says the trick is to balance the medicine, to give me enough so I don't ever hear the snap but not so much that I'm a zombie. 'I don't like to make people into zombies,' he told me one time, and I told him, 'That's good, because I don't like to be a zombie either.'"

"Why didn't you turn Father Coonie in?" I asked.

"Nobody would have believed me," he replied. "I didn't know if I believed myself. If I could go crazy on the spur of the moment, I could imagine things that didn't happen. And besides, even if it happened the way I remembered it, it had to be my fault somehow. That's how we all feel," Larry said. "It's our fault, not the fault of the Father Coonies of the world. Even other people think that way. They say things to you like, 'What did you do to encourage him to do that?' "

"So you owe the little man," I said.

"I owe him a lot."

"The time may come when you can pay him back," I said.

"I hope so," Larry said. "I'd give anything for that to happen."

# 31

# In the Administration Building

## SATURDAY, JANUARY 23, 1954

arry had been wrong about one thing. The Sunrise police were at the hospital bright and early Saturday morning. They wanted to grill Harry.

"He had an altercation with Kurt Harrison," they told the little man. I heard all this from a friendly employee later.

"Not an altercation," the little man replied. "He just acted out . . . if it really happened."

"Well, maybe he continued acting out by calling friends in Sunrise and having them beat Harrison to a pulp," the tall, thin policeman said. There were two cops, the tall, thin one and a more ordinary-sized one who was very quiet.

"Patients don't have access to telephones," the little man replied.

"Yeah, and I can jump over the Empire State Building too," the angry cop shot back.

"No one talks to a patient without contacting a legal guardian first," the little man said firmly. "Also, I'll have to see your warrant to let you visit Harry."

"Have it your way." The other cop was angry now. As they both stalked off, it was clear that once they got the warrant, they would be harder on Harry because of the little man.

## 32

# From the Little Store

SATURDAY, JANUARY 23, 1954

hen I thought about it, I decided I needed to know more about Father Coonie. To me, the major question now was: How did Kurt Harrison get to know Father Coonie?

I found the answer through Nancy Jane and then through the police.

When I called her, I asked if she could get the white-haired editor of *The Sentinel* out to talk to me. "Probably," she said. "He and I are friends."

"We came today," she said that afternoon, "because Red has an appointment out of town tomorrow. They put the paper to bed about noon on Saturdays. It's the Sunday edition, but they finish it by noon today and deliver it on Sunday morning."

"I want to make a little deal," he told me. "If you find out something I can use, I want to know it." He seemed so intense.

"OK," I said. Some things are easy. It is easy to promise something you don't have. Then if you ever get it, you can decide whether you really have it or not, whether or not to share it with the "promised" person.

"Tell me about Father Coonie," I said.

"He was in Sunrise in the early nineteen thirties. He'd been in a lot of different churches. I learned later they were moving him around. He'd be someplace for a while—at first the people loved him, thought he was the most holy and perfect man they ever knew—and then he'd get in trouble and they'd send him elsewhere."

"But the bishop knew what was going on?" I asked.

"Someone in the upper echelons did. I doubt it was the bishop. After Sunrise, they sent Coonie to the seminary." Red's face darkened. He seemed very much involved in all of this.

"Did you have contact with him when he was here?"

"No, not the way I think you mean. My contact with Coonie was as an adult, as a parishioner and a reporter, not as an altar boy. As it all came down, I knew what he was doing pretty soon after it started leaking out—that was a couple of years into his ministry here—but I didn't report it or try to do anything about it. And he just kept on screwing little boys."

We all seek our ways to repent, don't we? If you're a reporter and you don't write the story when you should, even though you know it and think you can find the sources for it, and even though to write it might destroy you, you probably live the rest of your life looking for another chance to write it.

"Where was the seminary?" I asked.

"That seminary down there on the lake."

"To get some kind of an advanced degree?"

"To be a teacher, assistant professor of prayer and worship or something like that."

"The fox among the chickens," I said, not with a smile but with a deeper anger than anyone could really understand.

"It didn't turn out that way," Red said. "Somehow he changed.

119

I kept track of him. He has been my nemesis since this whole thing began."

"He changed?"

"My guess is that he developed a long-term relationship. I've never known it to happen. Rape is rape, whether you are raping someone of the same sex or of the opposite sex. I didn't think it was possible for someone to quit being a rapist to have a different relationship instead, but maybe that's the case."

"How long did he stay at the seminary?"

"Until he retired. Until he went to the old priests' home. Of course, he went a lot earlier than many would. That's one thing the hierarchy finally did. They retired him early."

"But by that time, he wasn't a threat to anyone?" I asked.

"That's what I was told, and I kept track," he said. "He messed up a lot of people's lives." Red was obviously obsessed with Father Coonie. He had never lost track of Father Coonie. After Coonie, all Red's journalistic life was probably lived knowing that everything he covered was no story at all compared to Father Coonie. Sometimes lost opportunities can't be recovered.

"I'll do what I can to get the story for you," I told Red as he was leaving. Somehow I didn't think I believed it, but right then it didn't seem so bad to let him keep on living with the illusion that lost stories can somehow be recaptured in the time to come.

## 33

# On the Ward

**LATE SATURDAY AFTERNOON, JANUARY 23, 1954**

The police came back, this time with a warrant. I learned later that they couldn't find any of Harry's relatives, so they just went to court and got some kind of special warrant instead.

"How come the hospital chaplain Father Hogan called Kurt Harrison so much?" they asked Harry, as if he had some way of knowing. They told Harry the phone calls were from Hogan's house, not from the hospital. They didn't tell Harry how they knew this happened.

"I don't know," Harry said. He hardly had any contact with Hogan at all.

"We think the two of you were in collusion," the young cop said ominously. "We think it has to do with Father Coonie. We think it ended up with Kurt Harrison being beaten." He kept harping on it, but what could Harry say? It was a crazy idea that didn't make any sense at all, but the cops had to be doing something, I suppose.

· · ·

Harry told me this himself. He said after the cops left the little man just shook his head and said, "Sometimes I think it's folks like that who need to be committed." Then, he told Harry his confinement to the ward was over.

# 34

# The Chapel

SUNDAY, JANUARY 24, 1954

Y ou're the one who introduced Kurt Harrison and Father Coonie," I told the hospital chaplain Father Lucian Hogan when I saw him in the chapel late Sunday night. We just sat there in the front pew and talked with Jesus listening. At least that's what Father Hogan must have thought, since he thought Jesus was right there in the tabernacle.

Father Hogan looked straight at me. His eyes were deep pools of blue light even in the dimness of the chapel. His face was older now, but it had surely been both beautiful and very young once.

"I'm just guessing. You can deny this. You met Father Coonie in the seminary. You were a student there, and he was some sort of teacher.

"This is an even wilder guess. You both had the same proclivities, and you found out you could love each other without having to hurt anyone else."

Hogan didn't drop his head. He listened without moving.

"For some reason or other, when Coonie wanted access to

this institution, you didn't think you could give it to him. You introduced him to Kurt Harrison instead."

"Mitch wouldn't let me get the key," Father Hogan said. "That's his name. Father Mitchell Coonie. He wouldn't let me be the one to get the key. He said he loved me too much to put me at risk.

"The last few years, Mitch has been slowly going crazy, senile dementia. Finally, he became convinced everyone knew about him and how he caused Marcia Weinhart to be murdered. For some reason, he had at least fifty copies of that old paper with the story of her death in it. He sent clippings everywhere, and then he got it into his head he needed to talk to everyone he'd wronged.

"I don't know why I'm telling you all this," Father Hogan added.

I waited.

"What happened to him?" Father Hogan asked. "It's been more than two weeks since I've seen him." So now I knew why he was telling me all this.

I didn't answer.

"Kurt was always struggling for money, and Mitch had more money than he knew what to do with. I used the phone from home to put the two together. That way people didn't see me talking with Harrison here at work.

"When Mitch went AWOL, I called Kurt, but he wouldn't tell me anything. He said he was in the dark just like I was. He didn't know what happened to Father Coonie."

"You hired the folks to try to beat the information out of him?"

"Lord, no!" he said. His very reaction made me believe him. "I desperately wanted to know where Mitch was, what had happened to him, but I've never hurt anybody or asked someone else to hurt them. I just wouldn't do that."

I believed him. In fact, I saw him as a sort of savior. I suspected he had led Mitchell Coonie down a different and much better path. The only problem was, the damage had been done. It couldn't be reversed. The evil was alive, and it would finally grow to engulf them all.

"Somehow or other, the police know about your phone calls to Kurt Harrison," I told Hogan. "They'll be talking to you. You'd better have your words in order."

At least, I could give him that much warning.

# 35

# The Administration Building

## SUNDAY, JANUARY 24, 1954

I tried desperately to rectify the error I had made. "Who is on the telephone from that office at this time of night?" the operator's voice broke in. I was in full panic, and she was in her "I'm the one who runs the switchboard" mode.

I just hung up. I tried again from another office. "Who is trying to call out?" she asked. "It's two A.M. If you don't tell me who you are, I'll call security." Security was a sixty-year-old man who limped around and checked the elevators.

Finally, I just went and pleaded with her. "I need to make a phone call out," I said. "It's a life-and-death matter."

"Listen, friend," she said, using what was her almost always wicked smile. "The man who claims to be the boss around here may think you're Roy Rogers, but I know you're just Roger Storr. That's your name. It's Roger Storr. You're not anyone who really matters."

No matter what I did or said, she wouldn't listen to me. She refused even to let me call the little man. I think I could have convinced him.

To this day, I can't understand why she didn't turn me in for being in the offices at night, but she didn't. Maybe she enjoyed lording it over me too much. She knew if she turned me in, I could be permanently grounded and she might not get another chance to lord it over me.

In any case, I didn't get to make the call.

That night Father Lucian Hogan was murdered in his bed.

It was that night the demons started coming at me again. They would keep coming until the whole thing was over. And sometimes, they would tie me in knots.

# 36

# In Front of the Willow Tree

MONDAY, JANUARY 25, 1954

They tied him to his bed and tortured him before they murdered him," Nancy Jane said. "Evidently, they just walked up and rang the doorbell. When he came to the door, they forced him back inside, overpowered him, tied him up, and tortured him with a knife. Finally, they killed him. Red told me it was none too soon."

I wanted to cry. "Whoever it was, they beat Kurt Harrison to find out about Mitchell Coonie," I replied. "They found out about Father Hogan too."

"There was nothing you could do about it," Nancy Jane said.

"There might have been, if I was quick enough," I said.

"I used to have a friend who told me, 'Never *should* on yourself,'" she replied. "It's easy, when things are already over, to think you should have done something."

"And it's easy, when you're not the person who messed it up, to make some kind of excuse for a dumb ass who did," I told her bluntly.

She shut up.

"This morning, all hell broke loose around here," I told her. "The little man called me in and told me, 'Listen, Roy. This is not a game now. If you know something about this, tell me and I'll tell the police.'

"I told him I didn't know anything. I said just because I was Roy Rogers didn't mean I knew who murdered anybody. Or anything else about the process either.

"The little man was more upset than I've ever seen him," I told Nancy Jane. "He told me, 'The whole future of this institution is involved now. People think we kill folks in the tunnels,' referring to a rumor that had gone around a few years back. 'They want to think we cover up all kinds of terrible things. It breaks my heart. All we're trying to do is to help the very people the community has thrown away.'

" 'There are good people and bad people everywhere,' I told him. 'Why should that be any different here?' But he was heartbroken.

"He just wouldn't leave it there," I told Nancy Jane. "He kept on trying to press. The hospital is the little man's life. He has tried to help people no one else would ever try to help. He succeeds sometimes and fails sometimes, but he always works against great odds."

"And you're adding to the problem," she said. "You're holding back on things he needs to know."

"I can't tell him what I know. That would only make things worse," I said, and all of a sudden I became aware of what a responsibility it is to be someone like Roy Rogers.

# 37

# The Blacksmith Shop

MONDAY, JANUARY 25, 1954

L isten, Hoss," I said. "I don't care what you can't talk about. There's been a murder now. I need to know."

Hoss looked at me in the glow of the forge. It was a dull, gray day outside. In the brick blacksmith shop, the room itself was dim and burnt-iron smelling like it always was. Hoss was alone, beating some glowing iron on the anvil. The clinks echoed through the old building. Even on a cold day like this, sweat rolled from his brow. His blue work shirt was rolled up to the elbows, and his old overalls (with all their little burned places) sagged. Hoss was more aware than he appeared to be. He knew about the turmoil in the hospital.

He tried to pull a Harry on me. "You know they won't sell you overalls at the commissary now?" he said. We didn't really buy things from the commissary. They were issued, but we got to choose. Like I told you before, it was a part of our greater freedom lately.

"Why did Coonie want to see you?" I asked, ignoring Hoss'

attempt to change the subject. And then I added, "Or what did he say to you when he got to see you?"

"He asked me to forgive him," Hoss replied. He quit beating on the iron. As he stood there, the red glow left the piece of iron. It became inert.

"He told me he caused a murder way back when, and then he said he needed my forgiveness. He was crazier than I am. He wasn't making any sense at all."

I was flabbergasted. The blacksmith had become a veritable fount of words. "He said he would send me a clipping about the murder, and I told him that I didn't want his clipping!"

I started to interrupt, but Hoss just barreled on: "Coonie said he needed God's forgiveness before he died. He said he had some kind of terrible illness. He said he had turned over a new leaf, been a different person for a long, long time. He said he wanted my forgiveness too.

"I just told him he could go to hell."

I waited. When Hoss didn't go on, I said, "He raped you." Somehow it didn't seem right. Hoss would have been too old.

"No. He raped my ten-year-old son. His name was Hoss too. My Hoss committed suicide when he was seventeen."

"What year was that?" I asked.

"Hoss was raped in 1928. He committed suicide in 1935."

"You didn't live in Sunrise?"

"No," and he named another town. Then he added, "They didn't do anything to Coonie. They just sent him off to Sunrise. At the time, I wanted to kill Coonie. I was looking for him, but then I broke down completely.

"This time when I saw him, I knew he was suffering more alive."

"How did you end up here?" I asked. I couldn't believe they'd send him to Sunrise with Father Coonie in the town.

"At first, they sent me to another mental hospital clear across the state. When Coonie left Sunrise and they thought it was safe, they transferred me here. It's closer to home."

I waited.

"I've said the last I'm gonna say," he said. "I only said it for the little man. The little man's OK, even if he don't believe in overalls. I don't want him to get in trouble." Then he shut up. I never again heard him mention a word about what had happened to him or to his son.

# 38

# Out and Around

## LATE MONDAY AFTERNOON, JANUARY 25, 1954

Harry and I got Bullet and we went out and around. We went down to the park, being careful to skirt the chicken farm. I could visualize Bullet taking after chickens.

"It just gets worse and worse," Harry said as we were walking. "Now Father Hogan has been killed. I liked Father Hogan."

"We need to be careful not to tell anybody about Pat's friend," I said. "Right now that would be the most wrong thing we could do."

"I know," Harry said, and, as it turned out, he did.

When we took Bullet back to Dr. Jane's and returned to the ward, the police were waiting. It was the same two cops—the quiet one and the tall, thin, bitter one. They latched on to us both.

They left me sitting in the outer room while they gathered around Harry in an adjoining room as if he were the murderer himself. They left the door open, on purpose of course, so I could hear.

"Somehow or other, you're a link in all of this," the more quiet of the two policemen told Harry as kindly as he could. No more bullying, at least to start. "You spit on Kurt Harrison. Whatever might have caused you to do that could have had to do with Father Hogan."

"Kurt Harrison is a bad man," Harry said.

"And Father Hogan?"

"I liked him. I didn't know him very well, but I'm sorry he was killed."

"You didn't know him very well?" The quiet cop sounded skeptical.

"I don't go to the tunnel church," Harry said. "I don't go to church at all."

"Listen, Harry," the policeman said. "We think there's a connection between what's happening in Sunrise and this place out here. We think you can break that open for us. If you don't tell us, things will be a whole lot worse."

"The tunnel church is crazy," Harry said. "They believe in transisubstitution."

I could have died! Where on earth did Harry ever hear of transubstantiation, the idea that when the priest says his prayer, the bread and wine become Jesus?

"Give it up," the thin cop said bitterly. "You can't talk to him. He's an idiot. We'll have to find another way."

"Transisubstitution don't make a whole lot of sense to me," Harry said. I was never more proud of him than I was that day.


That night, I heard there was to be a special legislative visit. The Sunrise police chief had called a friend in the legislature and told him someone at the hospital was involved in covering up a murder.

The head cop's friend contacted the Speaker of the state House of Representatives, who formed an emergency legislative committee to make an official visit, in other words, to come and put the pressure on big-time. They did that kind of thing—trying to apply pressure—a lot.

The legislature appropriated the money for the hospital. They were to be here by the end of the week, probably Thursday, if they could get their act together by then.

Then, after I heard that, I saw a copy of *The Sunrise Sentinel.* "Heinous Murder in Sunrise," the huge headline read.

The story told about Father Hogan and described his wounds. "The police have several leads," the story said without directly quoting the police chief. "An unnamed source is quoted as saying that there may be a connection between the murder of Father Hogan and events involving Father Mitchell Coonie that occurred in Sunrise almost twenty years ago. The police had already been looking into the mysterious disappearance of Coonie. *The Sentinel* is pursuing that aspect of the story."

That's the first time I had ever been called "an unnamed source," even if I was just an unnamed source in a roundabout way.

And to top it off, there was a sidebar. That grayed-in section of the page talked about Hogan's work as a chaplain at the hospital, said Hogan had requested long-term chaplain work instead of work in the regular pastorate. Hogan had ended up being assigned to Sunrise. According to the bishop, Hogan had requested someplace else, but when he was assigned to the Sunrise State Hospital, he had "obeyed the bishop as he had vowed to do."

Almost everything about the sordid story somehow touched the Sunrise State Hospital.

Without a doubt, the little man would spend a sleepless night worrying about the implications of the story in the newspaper,

135

and as it finally turned out, he had good reason not to rest easy. All kinds of forces were already arrayed against him and all he stood for. The time would come when the Sunrise State Hospital would be gone. It would be not just closed but mostly torn down.

That time came years later, but it had already started happening back then. The people of Sunrise had thrived on the hospital, been made much more prosperous than they would otherwise have been because of its large payroll, but they had never liked the hospital. It wasn't uptown enough for them. They always wished it were some kind of permanent manufacturing plant or something. They wanted something more reputable, so to speak.

When the time came they could get manufacturing plants, they encouraged the state legislators who wanted to close the hospital. Then when the manufacturing plants they brought in closed to send high-paying jobs to lower-paying places overseas, Sunrise was left with much less payroll, and those same people screamed bloody murder.

But of course, the legislators were glad to be encouraged. The legislators wanted to close state mental hospitals to save money, to put the mentally ill out into the community, meaning into nursing homes and under bridges.

The legislators promised more money to "community-based" mental treatment, but they knew they were lying. Once they didn't have those huge institutions, they would spend less and less until today the mental health system in this state is in a shambles. Many go untreated.

Don't get me wrong. State hospitals were far from perfect. They had all kinds of problems, some more than others, but no one has ever really cared for crazies anyway. Once there was some medicine that made it so us crazy folks didn't just have to be locked away, the rich and powerful began to think of other ways to use the money, so they closed the hospitals.

"Love of money is the root of all evil." Some book says that somewhere, and as crazy as a lot of other parts of that book might be, that line is right.

# 39

# In the Laundry

**TUESDAY, JANUARY 26, 1954**

ven back in 1954, there was not much contact between men and women patients. For obvious reasons, that kind of thing was strictly supervised. Fortunately for me, Rosalyn Pope worked in the laundry. She was one of those people the police had visited. Until then, I didn't know she had come from Sunrise.

Rosalyn was about twenty years or so younger than me. She had dark hair, this sort of narrow hatchet face, and large round glasses. I didn't like her very much.

The laundry was an interesting place. It was huge. It was brutally hot, even in the wintertime with the doors left partway open. There were a whole wall full of massive washers and another wall of huge dryers. I have no idea how many pounds of laundry they would hold. There were thousands of pounds of laundry done each day. You could even smell the steam from the steam pressers. It had the kind of acrid smell that ironing has, except more so.

There were two advantages to the laundry: It was loud. You

could talk to somebody with other people around and no one could hear you. And they were used to seeing me around. As long as I didn't talk to anybody too long, they didn't run me off. The people who knew me knew I wasn't trying to get it on with Rosalyn Pope.

"They must think there's a connection between the hospital and the events in town," I told her. "They must think you're a part of the connection." I didn't know what her connection was. All I knew was that she had come from Sunrise and that the police had interviewed her.

"No, I'm not," she said. "I don't know anything about what happened."

I wanted to say more, but I didn't have a pry bar to break her loose. Her arrogance made me think she was involved in this somehow, but whatever that involvement was, I wouldn't learn it right away. Rosalyn Pope had the upper hand.

# 40

# Two Conversations

**WEDNESDAY AND THURSDAY, JANUARY 27-28, 1954**

Over the next two days, I talked to two different people and they gave me two different stories.

When I talked to George Carson, I couldn't get him to say much except about Marcia Weinhart.

"Marcia Weinhart set up all those little boys," he said bitterly. "That's why she was killed."

"Why would she do that?"

"She had the hots for Father Coonie. She thought she could reform him."

"You know that for a fact."

"Marcia Weinhart was an older lady by the time Coonie came. She married late, in her thirties, and her husband died in a farm accident just five or six years later. He left her two young sons. Those sons were gone from home when Coonie came. So she had been alone for a while. She worked as an operator for the local phone company, if I recall. She was poor as a church mouse. People said Father Coonie was a millionaire. The only thing Marcia Weinhart did that really mattered was putter around the parish. As she puttered, she wanted to putter with Father Coonie."

"So somebody killed her because she set their son up?"

"That's what I believe," George Carson said. "You're supposed to be some kind of genius, what with your being Roy Rogers and all. Surely you had that figured out by now."

"I thought I did," I said, "but you can never be too sure. You can never be too sure."

Larry from the lockup had a different story. "Marcia Weinhart was an innocent bystander in everything she did," he said. "She had set up the altar schedule for the last ten thousand years. You know how it is? Someone takes something over in the church, and that becomes who the person is. They wouldn't give it up if they were dying."

I did know how it is. My father had been the altar sexton in his church seemingly forever. He would have killed before he gave it up.

"Marcia Weinhart was destroyed by what happened to me and all the others," Larry said. "Somehow, she found out about it early on, before most others knew. She just fell apart. She hadn't had anything to do with it, but she felt guilty for it. She came to my parents and told them how sorry she was. She had no idea what Coonie had been doing." As tough as Larry was, it was clear he had a soft spot in his heart for Marcia Weinhart. "In some ways, she was the most wronged person of all in this," he said.

Given what he had to face and what it did to him, I thought those words had power in them.

Larry's words helped me remember where I'd heard of Marcia Weinhart. Her name was buried in one of the hospital records.

The record room was filled with history if you could remember it all.

Marcia's name was on a form in a file folder that also had a little notebook in it. The notebook was simply dated 1918, no month or day.

It was written by a staff doctor. There was a picture of him in the records. He was a big bull of a man with stark, white hair.

> *People dying right and left [the notebook said]. High fever. Coughs, sometimes so bad the patient breaks a rib. Often presents as Hemorrhagic Pneumonia. Worst-affected patients turn blue and bleed from the ears, eyes, nose, and mouth.*
>
> *Some patients barely affected. Others suffering and dying. Hospital is at risk. Talking about closing down enclosed institutions such as this. They won't do it. What would they do with all these people?*

That little bit of the record led me to go to the hospital library and check out books about the flu epidemic of 1918. It didn't hit Sunrise, but evidently it did hit here in the hospital, probably because of someone they brought in from somewhere else. There was no way they could have closed this place back then. The outside world wanted all these people isolated here.

After I found this doctor's notebook in the record room, I walked out to the edge of the property. I walked through the cemetery again. The plat showed there was a whole section devoted to people who had died in 1918.

In a way, this cemetery was the most sacred place on all the grounds. It was an honor to have your body lying here. In 1918, many people claimed that honor.

According to the history books I read, worldwide more than 20 million people died of flu that year.

Epidemic flu spreads in an insidious way. The bad flu viruses combine with less bad ones, the ordinary flu we have each year. That makes the bad flu spread as if it were the less harmful kind. In a sense it disguises itself.

I remember as a young man walking in a public cemetery where we had some sort of relative buried. There was one section with whole families in it. Maybe a mother and five children. Or maybe a mother and father, with several children. You wondered what would happen to you if you were a small child and both your parents died.

No matter who your parents were or how they treated you, they were all you had. Good parents protected you from the evil of the world.

The protectors here were people like doctors, nurses, and attendants.

*Staff bailing out [the doctor's notebook said]. Only two doctors remain. Nurses will not come in to work. Attendants sparse. Only the poor work here now. Those who work here stay here. They don't go back in town. If you don't need what we pay to eat and live, you don't work here.*

*Epidemics and wars. The soldiers in them are the poor.*

But from what I could read in his own little notebook, that particular doctor hung in there. He worked night and day. "Some have talked about small mass graves," he wrote in the record. "Stood strongly against it. These people deserve their places too. They will have their places if I have to dig them myself."

But as the record went on, it became apparent he didn't have the strength to dig them. He hardly had the strength to treat the people whom he treated.

*Sometimes it is so discouraging [he wrote]. Nothing helps. Some medical authorities even write of going back to bleeding patients like they did of old. I can't think that would help. All I know is hydration and other kinds of palliative care are sometimes helpful.*

*Through it all, I think of my little daughter. She is not so little now. She is a beautiful woman and she means so much to me.*

His daughter seemed to give him strength. He could be so tired the cramped writing slanted down the pages going below the blue lines on the tablet, but when he wrote of his daughter the writing became stronger and more straight.

*Missed my daughter's birthday [he wrote].*

*Practice is failing. I knew when I came out here I would not be able to go back. Not until this whole thing is over. Still, you can't just let these poor people die.*

*Regular town patients have gone to other doctors, my wife Elsie says through letters. People come in and tell her, "I don't want to do it, but I have to leave the doctor."*

*She does not think they will return. The stigma of having practiced here in the epidemic will follow me for years, perhaps forever. She suggests we close the practice.*

So the old man had given up his practice in town to treat people here, probably for next to nothing. He was working day and night, and then it happened as you knew it would.

*I have symptoms now. I miss my family so, but cannot see them. Will never again see them. I must keep on treating people here. Even myself.*

*Meant to write my darling daughter. Meant to tell her how much she means to me. Meant to tell her to continue being the good person she has always been. She will do something great someday. She will bring a blessing to the world. . . .*

And then the writing stopped.

Later, there was a note in another handwriting:

*Dr. Horace Hopkins died in agony of the disease he had been treating in so many patients. By the time he died, he had pulled many patients who would otherwise have died and all of the affected employees through.*

*Visited with his daughter and read his last words to her. She wanted his notebook, but I told her there was too much risk of cross-contamination.*

*Town cemetery refused to take him. Threat of epidemic spread too great, they said.*

*Buried in the asylum cemetery among the ones he loved.*

According to a note I found in the record, the little notebook had been put into a safe in the superintendent's office. When it was found there years later by another superintendent, he put the notebook in the record. For some reason, he didn't contact the daughter to see that she got her father's notebook. That always seemed sad to me.

By the time Dr. Horace Hopkins died, the epidemic in the hospital was already burning itself out. The course of the disease was interesting, both locally and worldwide. It started slowly, flared up until people were dying even almost more quickly than you could get them to the infirmary, and then there was the burnout. People died so quickly, they couldn't pass the virus on. The next year, 1919, there was a smaller outbreak, and that went on for several years, each outbreak a little less than last year.

But all those dead were still lying in their graves, and all those children left without parents were still struggling, perhaps with grandparents, if they survived, or else God knows where. One of the ironies of the epidemic is that it was young adults who were hit worst. Older people often, but not always, avoided the disease or had lighter cases.

I knew one lady whose family lost her father. Because they were so poor, when the epidemic had subsided she was farmed out to work in other people's homes. In all her life, she never really spoke of that. The abuse and degradation was too great. She was always one who did what she had to do to survive. And she spent her life helping others.

So Dr. Horace Hopkins was the only employee ever buried in the hospital cemetery. He was buried there because, in serving as he did, he became one with those he served.

Marcia Weinhart was Dr. Hopkins' daughter. Her name was listed in the personal comments on a personnel form he must have had to turn in to come to serve and die here. That form was in the file.

All life is intertwining stories. No one is an island, as the poet said. Everybody's history is my own history, everybody's future my own future. There is no love but the love we share with one another.

Jesus told a story one time. I don't even know why I remember it. It was about a poor man lying destitute at a rich man's gate. The rich man never noticed him or fed him anything but garbage. As close as they were to one another, the gap between them was immense. The rich man wanted it that way.

When they both died, the gap remained, but this time, the poor man was on the good side of it and the rich man suffered.

God didn't make the gap. The rich man did.

# 41

## The Legislative Committee

### THURSDAY, JANUARY 28, 1954

The state legislative committee did come on Thursday. Not only did they come; they threatened to fire the little man. At least, that's what the rumors said.

I heard about it from my sources, but the word was also flying around the hospital as a whole. "The chairman of the committee was some kind of pompous ass," the employee I talked to said. "He called the little man in and shut the door, and when it was all over, word went around that if local authorities didn't quit complaining, the little man was out."

"I don't believe it," I told my source. "They may have said a lot of things, but I don't think they threatened to fire him. For one thing, he's got friends in the legislature. Those folks have crazy people in their families too. And for another, they can't replace him."

"You know that," my friend said, "but they may not," and I had to admit he could be right.

There was one thing about all this I didn't understand until later. The historical direction of the institution was already beginning to play out. It would take years to close the place, but several devious legislative types were already looking for ways to do that down the road. The little man knew that. Looking back on it, I know he knew it. And he knew the patients needed someone dedicated to keeping it alive and viable until that time came. He probably hoped he could do something to keep the hospital open, but he was paddling upstream.

More than thirty years after all this happened, I stood one day and watched them tear the whole place down, or at least most of it. No telling how many months it took to do that. That day, I watched the wrecking ball destroy everything, at least in bricks and mortar, that the little man had worked for. That's when it occurred to me that there are certain things which trump doing good. Money trumps doing good. Power trumps doing good. Getting more for yourself at the expense of others trumps doing good. Figuring out how to get ahead of other people, especially helpless people like the mentally ill, trumps doing good.

No wonder all us crazies are forgotten now. There are still some people running around trying to do good, but there are a whole lot more figuring out ways to take away the money used for mental health care. It was always that way. It is that way now, and it was that way when the legislative committee came to visit back in 1954.

Doing good doesn't protect you from anything.

Life is interesting. No matter who you are, some people like you and some people don't. For some people, the better you try to be to them, the more they hate you.

"That's just the way life is," the little man told me one time. "For one thing, Roy, it's a part of mental illness. Some mentally ill people latch on to you. They want you to do more for them than you can ever do. When you can't do it, they end up blaming

149

you, maybe even hating you. That's why psychiatrists are sometimes murdered."

"Then just don't help," I said.

"That wouldn't work. If I did that, I'd end up doing nothing," the little man said. "So what if somebody doesn't like you? It's OK. It shouldn't stop you from trying to do good things."

"I've got people burning up my phone lines," I was told the legislative chairman told the little man. "If you don't do something to get them off my butt, you'll pay. I promise you, you'll pay."

He probably did say that, and if he did, it just showed he valued something different than the little man valued.

Word shoots around a place like this. No sooner had the great committee left than Nevaeh was knocking on my door, so to speak. Someone brought a note with instructions to meet Nevaeh back near Hoss' tree. Nevaeh spent almost all her time outside. She loved this place. She loved the shelter and the soft bed, but she was basically a homeless person, someone who was meant to be outside.

"You gotta save this place, Roy," Nevaeh said. There was panic in her voice.

"I know," I said, trying to put her off.

"No, you don't. This place is a lifesaver. If I didn't have this place, I'd be dead by now."

"Not necessarily," I said.

"I ain't never had sex with nobody," she said.

"I wasn't asking you."

"Wiseass. When I was eight years old I decided I wouldn't have sex with nobody ever, not that they weren't already trying. I had already watched my mamma, and I knew what all that did to you.

"You know what that means out on the street—being young and not having sex with nobody? It means you don't have a protector. It means you have to fight the bastards off. You become a challenge to them."

"I never came on to them on purpose, Roy. I never taunted some big stud or wore short dresses with no panties, but still I had to fight.

"When Mamma died, I knew I was gonna have to live under bridges and around the stockyard forever, so I decided I wouldn't have sex with nobody. Not for anything. Not for food. Not for money. Not for booze. Not for cigarettes. I been beat up and almost killed, but I ain't given in.

"But it wouldn't have lasted," she said sadly. "There were always men who wanted me. And they were finally gonna get me. That don't happen here."

"Tell me about Marcia Weinhart, the real story."

"Jacqueline and I hitched down the highway toward this way and I got pneumonia. I was down there under the viaduct. Marcia found me there. That's where the paperboys threw the papers."

"Where the paperboys threw the papers?"

"They paid these little kids to throw the giveaway papers in the town. They threw a few, and then when they got tired, they just took the rest and tossed the bundles in the grass down by the viaduct. I would get a bundle and spread out the papers and sleep on them and under them."

"But you got sick."

"I was almost dead. I was staggering around. Marcia Weinhart was just driving by and found me. She really did. She saw me staggering around. She stopped her car and got out and took me in. Jacqueline hid and let her take me. Later when I came back, Jacqueline told me to go with Marcia.

151

"When she first found me, Marcia wanted to take me to the hospital, but I wouldn't go, so she took me home instead. She called some doctor who carried drugs around in the trunk of his car. He was a real doctor.

"He looked at me and gave me some medicine. After he left, Marcia told me he was a rich man. 'He makes it selling drugs out of the trunk of his car,' she said. She told me later, she meant drugs to patients. He was both their doctor and their pharmacist. I don't know why she thought I'd want to know that."

"What happened then?"

"I don't stay no place very long. That's why I'm still alive. I keep moving before they can move in on me. It's a hard life.

"That night, when I found Marcia dead on the altar of the church, I just ran away. I didn't talk to nobody, and I didn't never come back again until they brought me here."

"You weren't very old back then."

"No one believes a homeless person, especially a homeless kid. There wasn't nothin' I could do but run."

And then Nevaeh teared up. "I want to be buried in that old graveyard out there," she said, pointing toward the hospital cemetery. "I want a number on me just like all the others. I ain't been nobody all my life, and I won't be nobody when I'm dead, but I'll have a number on me and I'll be with my family here at the hospital. Aside from Marcia and Jacqueline and the old man who protected me, the little man and a few folks here are the only good people I ever knew."

"What if it doesn't happen that way for you?" I asked. "What if they do close the place down like you think they will?"

"I ain't goin' to no nursing home," she said. "They don't let you walk out on the grounds. If they try to take me there, I'm on the road again, no matter what."

"Nevaeh, did you kill Father Coonie?" I said quietly. She was an honest person. She would tell me the truth.

"No," she said. "I might have if I could've, but I didn't have the chance."

I believed her.

# 42

## Back to Larry

On Friday, I went to talk to Larry. It seemed to me like he would be a whole lot more help than George Carson would be.

"What's the connection between Rosalyn Pope and what happened to Marcia Weinhart?" I asked.

"None I know of," Larry said. He was fidgeting around, his eyes shifting back and forth. This might be the last time I could talk to him for a while.

"Rosalyn was just an ordinary girl, a teenager at the time. She was Adrienne Powell's daughter. She wasn't very smart, and she was troubled, even then, but she didn't have anything to do with Marcia or with Father Coonie. She didn't even go to the same church they did. I don't think she went to church at all."

"The police interviewed her when they came out."

"Probably just because she was from Sunrise. They may have thought anyone from Sunrise was fair game. She was too young to have really been involved."

"I'd hoped for something else," I told him.

"Visit with someone who has a view inside the cop house," Larry told me. "You have a lot of contacts. Find out that way."

At first that seemed impossible. Then it occurred to me, there might just be an outside chance. At least, it wouldn't hurt to try.

# 43

>─┤─◆╲─❂─╱◆─┤─<

# Back on the Ward

**FRIDAY, JANUARY 29, 1954**

ometimes the strangest things set Larry off. When he got back to the ward that morning, he picked up a *TIME* magazine. There was a little article in it that said Senator Joe Mc-Carthy's popularity was climbing. More people were in favor of the Communist-witch-hunting bigot and what he was doing than ever before.

"And they say I'm crazy!" Larry started shouting. "Bigots run the world. They rape little boys, and they say I'm crazy!" He was flailing now.

Larry was doing what I sometimes did. He was letting something in the world set him off. I never knew for sure whether that happened just because it happened or it happened because people like me and Larry wanted it to happen. I didn't know whether Joe McCarthy was a reason or an excuse.

The attendants moved in on Larry immediately. They tried to be as gentle as they could. One time they hadn't been, and there was real trouble. An attendant lost his job for it.

"I was raped by Joe McCarthy," Larry was shouting by the

time they got him under control. They didn't use straightjackets like they used to. If they could get it down you, they used medication instead, but that took time to work. Sometimes that was good, but sometimes it just robbed you of who you were.

By the time they got Larry settled down, he was saying, "I see Joe McCarthy in my dreams." He was slurring his words. "I see Joe McCarthy coming at me. . . ." And then he described some things I wouldn't write here.

One thing I learned from Larry. Some stark-raving mad delusions are at least half-true.

By the time Larry drifted off, he was muttering, "Talk to the police. Tell the police I was raped by Joe McCarthy."

In later years, they'd have more specific names for Larry's illness, but it really doesn't matter what name you give it. His problems had a cause, or a multiple complex of causes, some from inside Larry and some outside. Larry was buffeted by winds beyond his choosing. I knew about that. Sometimes I was buffeted by those winds too.

"I get sad about what happens to Larry," Harry told me later. His employee friend had described the whole scene to him. Harry always told me what he learned. In fact, he told me in great detail. Harry could take an hour to tell a story it would take me five minutes to tell, but that was just the kind of person Harry was.

"Let's go out to the cemetery," Harry said.

"We could get Bullet and take him with us."

"Of course we could," Harry replied. "Bring your cemetery notebook with you when you come."

# 44

# Out to the Cemetery

**FRIDAY, JANUARY 29, 1954**

arry had someplace to go before we made our trip. I told
him I needed to go call Nancy Jane. Then I would meet him
in an hour, out by the blacksmith shop. From there we could
walk toward the county road that bordered the institution on
the east, walk north down that road, turn back on a road toward the west, and make our way to the cemetery.

When we met, Harry had his sack full of paper flowers.

"Putting those on people's graves just makes you look more
crazy," I told Harry.

"I'm not crazy. I've got friends out there, and you know
where they are," he said.

As we walked up the road, Bullet roamed the fields on either
side, crisscrossing back and forth. When we got to the cemetery,
the dog danced among the flat numbered markers, his red-blond
body shining in the sun.

"Where's Wallace Honniecutt?" Harry asked, and I told him.

"When I first came here, Wallace was the only one who'd

talk to me," Harry said. "One thing I try to do. I try to say hello to people when they come. I try to make them feel at home. I remember what Wallace did for me." He put two paper flowers on Wallace's grave, a blue one and a yellow one.

Harry was a one-man greeting committee. He had that reputation long before I knew him.

"Melissa Endicott was a friend of mine," Harry said as he put a red paper flower on her grave. "She came from Sunrise." That name vaguely rang a bell for me.

"And there's Laura Crain," he added. "She was from someplace else altogether."

It took more than an hour for Harry to distribute all his flowers. All the while, he told me of each person.

"We could go back by Bullet's little pond," I said. "See if his doghouse is still there."

Larry hung his head. "Bullet wouldn't like that. Bullet almost lost his life out there." Thank God Bullet was improving. We just didn't know how much he had improved.

"We'll go back the way we came," I said, and Harry shook his head.

"We could cut across the cow field," Harry said. "It's the short way."

"That's not a very good idea," I said, but almost before I got the words out, Harry had started walking through the pasture toward the cow field.

The cow field was the holding field where they kept the dairy herd. If you were going to go that way, you had to cross the field or go a long way around.

Harry was way ahead of me, Bullet dancing around his feet. When he got to the fence around the field, Harry lay down and rolled under. I always held down the top piece of barbed wire and crawled over. We're all different people.

Harry was about quarter way across the field and I was just coming across the wire when Bullet started barking at the cows.

Now I don't know if you know anything about cows or not, but they don't like dogs barking at them; at least these seemingly huge black-and-white Holstein milk cows didn't like Bullet barking at them. The little dog was dancing toward them and then back. You would never know he had been hurt. Surely he still felt pretty punk, but you couldn't tell it now. He was going to take on the whole cow herd.

First of all, the cows circled up, moving restlessly, their huge brown-black eyes fixed on the little dog. They seemed to be deciding what to do. They weren't deciding individually. They were deciding as a herd, a one-hundred-animal-strong herd.

About the time I got to Harry, Bullet charged the cows and they charged back. As they started coming, the dog started yelping and ran toward Harry, which meant, of course, the whole herd ran toward us.

By this time, we were running as fast as we could run toward the other fence. The dog was already under the wire and safe, but he didn't quit barking. When I thought about it later, I could see him smiling in his mind, thinking, *Suckers! You all fell for that.*

Harry rolled under, as easy as you please, and I tried to go over, but I got hung up on the barbed wire. As the cows came charging toward me, Harry pulled me and I heard a ripping in my overalls. That wasn't good. Overalls were a precious commodity nowadays. There was no doubt about it. After this, I would need another trip to the commissary, and I just had to pray they still had some overalls stuffed away.

I never told the little man, but I told the patients who helped in the commissary to cop onto some overalls and put them back. I hoped the patients had been able to do that.

"Well, we made it," Harry said, breathing hard. By this time, Bullet had wilted. You would have thought he was about to die. *Serves you right,* I thought toward the dog, but I didn't say it out loud because it would hurt Harry's feelings.

"We barely made it," I replied, and then I looked out in the field. There was my little cemetery book, lying in the middle of the field where it had fallen from my pocket. The cows had trampled it on their way toward us, and they would probably trample it or poop on it on their way back.

There was no way I was going back into that field to get my little book.

"They milk them in a couple of hours," Harry said. "We can come back then and get the little book."

"We won't bring Bullet," I said. "No telling what will happen if we bring Bullet."

"There won't be cows then," Harry said.

"No, Harry," I said unequivocally. "We take Bullet back to Dr. Jane."

When I got back my little book, I looked up Melissa Endicott. She was George Carson's sister.

# 45

## On the Ward

ardly had I gotten back than the little man accosted me. "The main herdsman called me. He was screaming into the phone at me. He said that when he got hold of you, he'd wring your neck."

I didn't say anything.

"He said it's not good to run the cows."

"He's quick," I said truthfully. "We just got back from there."

"He said they give less milk when you run them."

"I wouldn't know," I said.

The little man just laughed a little. "I told him that now maybe they'd give whipped cream instead. He didn't laugh. He slammed the phone down in my ear."

Actually, I didn't think it was very funny either.

"Melissa Endicott was your sister," I told George Carson later on that evening. "She was a patient here."

"Something happened in the family," George said. "It drove her crazy."

"You wouldn't tell me if I asked you?"

"No."

"How come she's buried in the hospital cemetery? She's got family in town. Your family would have the means to bury her."

"Missy wanted to be buried here," George said. "She said she was too good to be buried in the family plot."

"She must have been married at some time or other. She doesn't have your name."

"She was," George said. "Her husband left her."

"So now, she's buried with a number on her," I said.

"That's right," George Carson said. "She wanted it that way."

# 46

## Outside with Nevaeh

SATURDAY, JANUARY 30, 1954

aturday, I heard they had Larry completely down, so med-
icated he could hardly move. I hoped he wasn't having bowel
movements on himself. I hoped he was being able to keep his
dignity somehow. I even said a little prayer for Larry, though I
hardly prayed at all.

I never saw what good praying did. Either you did it yourself
or you figured out some way to get it done. Maybe God made
the world. I don't really know. But I sure know God doesn't
mess with the world now.

Later that day I ran across Nevaeh sitting on a bench under the
cyprus trees. "I have a question to ask you," I told her.

"Ask."

"Did you ever try to find out what happened to Marcia Weinhart? You said that when you found her murdered, you just ran
away."

"No, I never even wanted to find out," she said.

"Why not?" I asked. "She tried to help you. You ended up

back in Sunrise. I might have thought you would have looked into the whole thing."

"There warn't no percentage in it."

"What do you mean by that?"

"If she was dead, she was dead. When things are done, Roy, they're done."

"Weren't you just a little curious?" I asked. I couldn't understand it. I'd have been looking into it for sure.

"No. You only get in trouble when you get too curious," she said. "Father Hogan started to tell me about Marcia once, and I told him to forget it. I told him no matter what had happened, I didn't want to know, and I was right. I would have been better off not knowing."

"Let me ask you something else," I said.

"Shoot."

"They almost got you, didn't they?"

"What do you mean?"

"Someone attacked you and almost succeeded in raping you."

"A whole bunch of someones. You know how it is with homeless folks. Teenagers in packs go around attacking them. They think it's a sport. It's not always teenagers. I've had old men try me too, but this time it was teenagers.

"I had pneumonia. I couldn't hardly breathe. Those heartless bastards waited till I wasn't looking, and they surrounded me and held me down. They beat up the old Negro lady who was my friend. They beat her up and left her be. They didn't rape her because I was a handful enough. I had gone ape by then. They would have raped me and then killed me if they could of gotten away with it."

"The police intervened," I guessed.

"Intervened?"

"They broke it up."

"They broke it up. I never even knew why they were there. They took me in. They didn't do nothin' to the kids, of course. The kids all came from 'good' families, which means their parents were rich or on the city council or something like that.

"There was this cop. He was just a rookie. He had to be. He showed me some sympathy, and cops don't do that, not for people like me.

"He said, 'I know someplace they might take you in.'

"He didn't tell me this, but I heard about it later. He knew the little man. He grew up with the little man's son. He played around the little man's house. He called the little man sometime after midnight, I suppose, and the little man told him what to do to get me in.

" 'I knew he'd take you,' the cop told me. 'We have to do our court thing, but he's called the judge. I knew he'd take you. Even if he didn't have another place, he'd take you.' "

I just listened to Nevaeh.

"Have you ever seen your future flash before you, Roy?"

I just shook my head.

"When those horny studs were pawing at my clothes and trying to push a stick inside me, I saw my future flash before me. Even if I got out of this, I wasn't gonna be strong enough to hold them off forever. No one is. I seen others like me, and no matter how hard they tried or who tried to help 'em, finally, they all went down.

"I need this place. Don't let them take this place away from me." And she was gone.


"Someone says you're messing with the records," Harry told me. "Larry said to tell you some patients and employees met with the legislative committee and accused you of messing with the records. He said not to worry. It will be taken care of."

Harry looked away from me and then looked back. "For the life of me," he said, "I can't figure out how Larry does it! Just yesterday, I had heard they had him completely down."

I didn't tell Harry, but I wondered where Harry had heard the words "for the life of me." They weren't like Harry.

"The little man took the committee to the record room to show them what it's like," Harry said. "They wanted to look inside the records, and he wouldn't let them."

"He wanted to show them how secure the place is," I said. "He doesn't really believe I can do it, break in the record room, I mean."

"Kurt Harrison was there. He told those folks you have the little man wrapped around your finger. 'He's delusional,' Kurt Harrison said about you. 'He thinks he's Roy Rogers. He thinks no one holds a candle to him. He can go anywhere and do anything. That's what Roy Rogers thinks.' "

"Larry told you all of that?"

"He asked some of his friends to come and talk to me. His friends know everything."

"Larry's a good guy," I told Harry.

"And there's another thing," Harry said. "Larry's friends said to tell you that you have a lot of people on your side. They said there are a lot of patients who will do things for you. 'There are some who hate Roy,' Larry's friends said, 'and a whole lot who don't give a . . . ,' and then he used a nasty word like 'poop.' 'But there are a lot who will help Roy Rogers too.' "

Unless you told him not to, Harry would repeat anything.

"I guess Larry and his friends are on my side for sure," I said. "I'll bet his friends include some employees too, probably employees who were there when Marcia Weinhart was being killed in Sunrise."

Harry just ignored me. "They said to tell you the little man won't be talking to you about all this. He can't come to see you. That's what Larry's friends said. For him to come and see you would make it look like he's warning you. It would make it look like what they say is true.

"What's so important about the record room?" Harry asked. He was off on another tangent.

"It has all the history in it, Harry."

"All the history?"

"All the stories, Harry. Stories are important. They all intertwine." And then before Harry could ask what "intertwine" means, I held up my hand. "They all work together," I said. "One person's life touches another person's life, until finally, there's no telling who's connected."

"That don't make a whole lot of sense to me," Harry said.

"The time will come when the records will be considered the most important things of all," I told Harry. "This hospital has an emergency plan to save the records. I've read about it in the record room.

"They also have a plan for when this place will be closed down. I read that plan. That plan says: 'The time will come when patient records in a lot of institutions are strewn across the floors of rotting buildings. We don't want that to happen here.' "

"That won't happen," Harry said.

"The little man thinks it will. There are places like this all across the United States, in all kinds of towns and cities. The little man thinks they will be closed down."

"That would be terrible. Where would we go? Does he say why?"

"Money," I said. "He says it will finally occur to rich folks that they can save money by putting folks like us out on the street. He's passionate about it, Harry. He says he thinks it's bound to happen. 'They can turn these people out, claiming to provide better care, and then cut the benefits they themselves established, one little step at a time,' he said, and then, before he even finished his own sentence, the little man shut up."

"He shut up?"

"It occurred to him he was talking about me. People like him can find another job and another place to live. They have a place to go. He's a doctor. He can do all kinds of things. But folks like us . . ."

"Let's hope it don't happen soon," Harry said.

"Let's do what we can to keep it from happening right now," I told him.

"Larry said to give you this," Harry said, almost as an afterthought. He handed me a folded piece of paper. "He said he won't be able to help you for a while, but this might help. He said to tell you, 'Not everyone in that committee agrees with those who want to shut this whole place down.' "

Later, when I looked at it, I saw that the folded paper was a list of everyone on the legislative committee. It listed the names, the districts they represented, and the places where they lived—the hometown places.

There were some verbal messages Larry didn't want to send through Harry, I suppose, so he sent the piece of paper, and the piece of paper made it clear what I should do.

# 47

# In Front of the Willow and in the Record Room

## SUNDAY, JANUARY 31, 1954

osalyn Pope had an affair with Sonny Weinhart, one of Marcia's sons. That happened several years after Marcia Weinhart's murder," Nancy Jane told me that Sunday afternoon. "Red has a source in the police department. The police visited with Rosalyn because of Sonny."

"I wonder what kinds of things they asked," I mused. "George Carson told me Father Coonie and Marcia Weinhart were in cahoots. He said Marcia Weinhart helped set up those altar boys. But Larry from the lockup said that wasn't so."

"None of that has anything to do with the police," Nancy Jane said. "The police were just fishing. They tried to talk to everyone who came from Sunrise who seemed to be connected to Father Coonie or to the older murder. They had Father Coonie's notes which had his plans to visit certain people in the hospital. Coonie had a whole plan written out. He called it 'The Plan for Forgiveness.' He really seemed to think God had told him what to do."

"Was Rosalyn in Father Coonie's notes?"

"Red doesn't think so. He doesn't know for sure. His source

told him Coonie kept a diary, had for years. They were only given a few pages of it."

"By Father Hogan?"

"That's what Red thinks. He thinks that as time passed after Father Coonie dropped from sight, Hogan became more and more upset. He finally went to the police and told them Father Coonie was missing. He gave them some pages from Coonie's diary. Or if that's not the way it happened, maybe the police found the notes after Father Hogan's murder."

"What was the relationship between Hogan and Coonie?" I asked. "Specifically, I mean. I know what it was in general."

"They were a homosexual couple. They had been together regularly since seminary. They worked it out in several ways, since they never worked in the same parish together. Coonie was at the seminary all those years.

"Their relationship always involved traveling for one or the other of them. But when Coonie got older and retired, their relationship was more sporadic. Hogan and Coonie still seemed to love each other, but they just got together off and on.

"As far as anyone can tell, there was no more abuse of young boys once Coonie and Hogan met."

I didn't tell Nancy Jane how all that made me feel. I know the little man had told me I was supposed to be tolerant, but I still couldn't do that. I was still struggling with feelings of anger and despair. I still wanted to attack and kill homosexuals, though I knew I would never again do that. Not that I'd killed any, but that was just by the grace of God.

"By the time Coonie was trying to visit the people here, he was failing a lot," I guessed.

"He was in the early to the middle stages of some kind of dementia, according to the police. He cried a lot, and asked all kinds of people for forgiveness. He also had some form of epilepsy. He had terrible seizures. The epilepsy added to his innate depression."

"Epilepsy is a terrible disease," I said. I had watched the little man one time. We were at a cakewalk event where the hospital band was playing. He used to let me go with the band on things like that. I helped pack and unpack the instruments.

One of the people in the band had an epileptic seizure. The little man treated him. One thing the little man did was use a tongue depressor to keep the man from biting off his own tongue. That seems primitive now, very much not the thing to do, but back in 1954 it was a common action. The man had probably slipped a dose of medicine. We all did that once in a while. The medicine makes you drowsy or worse.

Anyway, if you did that and it caught up with you, the doctor had to try to keep your airway clear, keep you from swallowing your tongue, and just protect you until the seizure ended.

"What would have happened if you hadn't done that?" I asked the little man afterward.

"He could have died," the little man said. He still looked somewhat disheveled, but he was an amazing person. He truly wasn't much more than five feet, two inches tall and maybe 120 pounds or so, but when he needed to, he could summon uncommon strength. He must have had the strongest rush of adrenaline it was possible to have.

"Roy, what happened to Father Coonie?" Nancy Jane said suddenly. She caught me off guard.

I caught her drift immediately. "I didn't kill him," I told her quietly. "I wouldn't kill anybody." She knew how I felt about homosexuals.

"I know that, but . . ."

"Otherwise, I can't say much."

"Will we ever know?" she asked.

"Probably not," I said. "I can't see any way anyone will ever know."

"You're asking people to figure things out without having all the pieces of the puzzle," she told me.

"I have all the pieces," I replied. "I'll figure it out. I'm Roy Rogers."

It took two nights in the record room. The whole process was slowed because the old night watchman looked into the record room several times nowadays. There was no keeping on the light now. I had to sit behind the cabinets with a flashlight and then turn it off when I heard the door.

Of course, the night watchman didn't really look too hard. One time he had told me, "I won't catch you, Roy. I might know some of the things you do, but I won't catch you."

Anyway, the first night, I looked at record after record and didn't find what I was looking for. Several of the legislators had common names. There were all kinds of records with the same last name. And the connection, whatever it was, was likely to be buried in the smallest piece of paper. There wouldn't be a great big poster in the file that said: "This person is Representative So-and-so's great-aunt," or whatever.

Still, Larry was smarter than I am. It should have occurred to me that what the little man calls mental illness has no respect for class or wealth or race. You can be the richest, most powerful, most esteemed son of a bitch in the whole damned state and still have a crazy son or daughter or a raving wild-eyed great-grandmother. In fact, it's bound to happen.

He'd never told me this, but when I thought about it, I expected the little man got all kinds of calls from powerful people who needed his help in covering up the "dread disease" in their own families.

Anyway, mostly because I wasn't very smart, I didn't find the smoking gun the first night. But on the second night I did. And when I found it, I found not one connection but three. One legislator on the list had three people in the records. If I had quit looking when I found the first one, I'd not have found the others, but I didn't quit. Roy Rogers never quits.

Surely that person had a vested interest in seeing this place stay open, almost no matter what. I'd have to see.

# 48

# Outside the Laundry

**MONDAY, FEBRUARY 1, 1954**

Monday morning, I visited Rosalyn Pope. We were standing outside the laundry before she went to work. She was wearing a loose, faded flowered dress. She was angry with me.

"You know what happened to Father Coonie," she said. "You found him and you took him somewhere."

"You know how he died," I shot back.

"He deserved to die."

"I'm not arguing that, I suppose. Did you kill him?" I doubted she did.

"I didn't kill him, and I ain't saying no more about it."

"I ain't either," I mocked her. She knew better than to use "ain't." For her it was an affectation.

"But you gotta problem, don't you?"

I just listened.

"Unless you tell somebody you found him in the record room and hid him, there's not much you can do or say."

"I have a feeling you have a problem too. Since he hasn't

been found, he hasn't been shamed. If you wanted to make a big deal about his death and about everything he did, you failed."

"He deserved to die," she said, "but it didn't happen like you think it did."

"Your boyfriend killed him, or he knows who did." I thought maybe I could shake her loose.

"Sonny don't know nothin' about what happened to Father Coonie, and he ain't my boyfriend anymore. Ain't been for a long, long time. He just used me up and threw me away.

"Besides," she added, "you've got a bigger problem than I do. I hate the little man. Sometimes I think he can see right through me. He tells me things I don't wanna hear. If he goes down in all of this, so much the better.

"But it's not that way with you," she said smugly. "You worship the ground the little man walks on. You think he's a saint, a perfect person. You don't see that he's just a pompous piece of crap. What with his fancy suits and shirts, he don't give a shit about Rosalyn Pope. He just gives a shit about his favorites.

"He's goin' down," she said. "He's goin' down big-time, and you can't stop it. Because you can't tell folks about Father Coonie, you can't stop it. That just makes me bust with pride."

We were at an impasse, Rosalyn and me. But we were at a crossroads too. In a way, it reminded me of the Roy Rogers TV show I'd seen just last week. The bad guy used his grandson to try to drive Roy Rogers away from the mine the bad guy was trying to steal.

We have a way of using those around us for our own purposes. I just didn't know what Rosalyn Pope's purposes could really be.

That afternoon, I heard that the little man had been called to the central office in Jefferson City. He went there all the time, of course, but this time, it probably meant he was hip deep in doo-doo.

As soon as I heard about the trip, I went to talk to Alice. She was one of the toughs who had attacked Nevaeh, the one who thought she was George Carson's girlfriend. "The hospital records say your brother's in the legislature," I said. I was going to ask her to use her connections to protect the little man, but she was way ahead of me.

"That's why you don't have to worry about the little man," she said. "My brother likes him, and he's not the only politician who does."

"It helps to have someone powerful on your side," I said.

She grimaced. "My brother used his influence to put me here." Alice was dumpy but strong. When she looked at you, she seemed to see into your soul. She had the most piercing and troubled eyes.

"If you hate your brother so much, why didn't you call him out when the legislative committee came through your ward the other day?"

"My brother was ready for me. He knew I might raise some kind of stink," Alice said.

"Your brother sent word to you," I guessed. "He called you on the phone or had some friend talk to you before he came."

"Of course. He did both. He called on the phone and he sent a legislative staff member to visit. He told me that if I ever wanted to get out of here, I'd better keep my mouth shut. He said the little man was on my side, not his. The little man was working to try to get me well."

"And you believed him?"

"What could I do? If I ratted him out . . ."

She left the sentence unfinished, but what she meant to say was that if she ratted out her brother, she would be here "till the last dog died." She'd never have a chance of leaving.

177

You know what? I may be Roy Rogers, but even I have things to learn. That day I learned something I never would forget.

This was back at the time when people were ashamed of mental illness. (I suppose they still are.) Anyway, one reason the little man had so much power in the legislature and with some others was that the families of the rich and powerful people get sick too. The little man cared for folks in those families, sometimes "discreetly." In other words, he helped the hotshots get the crazy people in their families committed without any big thing being made about it. As a result, he knew a lot that powerful people didn't want revealed and he could be trusted to keep it confidential. So Alice's brother and the other people like him owed the little man.

It always bothered me that mental health care involved so much politics, but that's what I liked about the little man. He used the politics, but he helped the patient. He would help Alice, no matter what.

It's hard to believe anyone would be that selfless, but that's just how he was. One time he told me, "You need to focus on the right thing, Roy. That's your problem. You focus on the wrong things. You believe you can overcome your demons by beating homosexuals. It won't work. Violence and anger just feeds the demons, makes them stronger."

"What will work?" I asked.

"I can't tell you," he said. "You have to find that for yourself."

"You're a lot of help," I told him, but as it turned out, he was.

"Your brother's a powerful person," I told Alice that day.

"He'd be less powerful if people knew he had crazies in his family," Alice said. "That's death for a politician, and he's a politician. They say he might be governor or even a federal senator one day."

"But still you went to the legislative committee and complained."

"I told them you sneak into the record room," she said proudly. "It wasn't much, but at least I told them that." Alice had her pride. She wasn't going to let her brother back her down all the way, so instead of taking into her brother or the little man, she took into me.

But her anger at me was ironic. After all, it was Alice who brought herself to *my* attention, not the other way around. She talked to *me* about George Carson. And it was after that I went to the record room and looked her up.

Now I knew her inside out. While there might be some people who had been trapped at the Sunrise State Hospital just the way she claimed to be, she wasn't one of them. She had lived in squalor, a hopeless alcoholic. Her own crazy behavior—standing drunk on barroom tables and exposing everything she had—just embarrassed her family until they couldn't stand it anymore, so they had her committed. They were probably sick of trying to figure out ways to keep the newspapers from writing about how State Senator So-and-so's sister had been arrested for the sixth time for indecent exposure.

With each arrest, they were pressing their luck a little more. Without doubt, the time would come when some newspaper would break the story and some editorial writer would muse aloud about why Alice always got off scot-free when others didn't. "Could it be because she has relatives in high places?" the editorial would ask.

Needless to say, questions like that made for bad politics.

Again, you have to remember things were different back in the 1950s. Newspaper reporters didn't go out of their way to report the personal lives of politicians like they do now. They might report something terrible about you, John Q. Citizen, why you were

179

admitted to the hospital, for example, but by and large they left politicians and their lives alone. If I recall, open political reporting started with Wilbur Mills and Fanne Fox. Before then, newspapers and TV stations were at least somewhat inclined to let politicians' personal lives be private and personal. Everything changes, doesn't it?

So Alice was a hopeless alcoholic, but that was never publicly reported.

And though she hated it here, she was blessed. The little man was good at working with alcoholics. He always said it was a percentage business, but still he tried to help you become a part of that small percentage who stayed sober.

"Dedicated alcoholics will lie to you without flinching," he told me once. Then he told me that if you could help a small percent hit bottom and pull themselves out of it, you had done your job. "Never give up on anyone," he said, "and try not to let them give up on themselves."

"My brother's a sneaky SOB," Alice said. "He's gonna make it so they can't close this place, no matter what."

"How so?" I asked, but she didn't answer.

A few days later, I picked up a newspaper and there was a story about how her brother had drafted a bill requiring full state support for every patient moved from a mental hospital to private care, support that increased with inflation.

He had called all the mental health advocate groups in the state. He got them helping with the writing of the bill. He planned to introduce the bill when the legislature convened, and there was at least some hope it would pass.

"His bill makes this place look cheap," I told Alice when I saw her next.

"I told you he was a sneaky son of a bitch," she said.

"And then a few years later when they want to close the place, they rescind the bill," I said.

"Of course," she replied.

But we were both wrong. The bill didn't pass, and a few years later they closed the place just like they had planned to do all along.

At the beginning of all this, I told you I learned something that day. Really I learned two things. First, power speaks. There's always a roundabout or sneaky way to accomplish something, especially for a powerful politician. But the second thing I learned was more important. Money speaks louder. The money wanted this place closed, and though it took awhile, finally it was closed.

When they finally let Alice out, I heard she went back to drinking and standing on bar tables with her skirt up just like always.

# 49

> ━┼━❯━━◯━━❮┼━❮

# In My Secret Hiding Place

**TUESDAY, FEBRUARY 2, 1954**

uesday afternoon I received Adrienne Powell's diary in the mail. You might remember, Adrienne Powell was Nancy Jane's friend, the one who had known Marcia Weinhart.

The diary came in a brown envelope about four by six inches or so. It was written in strange purple ink, in a little bound book with purple flowers printed on the front. There was no return address and no indication where it came from.

When I saw what it was, I slipped it in my pocket. I didn't want anyone else to know I had it, and I didn't want to leave it where someone else could find it. Whoever sent it was trying to blow this whole thing wide open.

Adrienne Powell was Rosalyn Pope's mother. Her son was the state representative from a neighboring county where he had moved to start a business. Insofar as I knew, Adrienne was still alive, but, of course, much older.

The little book contained notes from about two years, including notes written at the time Father Coonie was relieved of his job in Sunrise and sent to be a seminary professor. It also dealt with the death of Marcia Weinhart. I wondered if maybe after that Adrienne didn't just quit writing.

Even at a glance, I could tell that until the Marcia Weinhart–Father Coonie thing, most of what Adrienne wrote was simply factual. "Warm today. Rain expected. This year is Irving Berlin's twenty-fifth year of writing songs. I love his song 'Always.' It was written about ten years ago for Ellin Mackay, who he later married."

And a little later: "Father Coonie is teaching people to write diaries. He calls them spiritual journals. He says they are quite important. He says if there was one thing he would teach every seminary student, it would be to keep a spiritual journal. I don't have the heart to tell him I've been doing it for years except that mine's not very spiritual."

As soon as I started reading Adrienne Powell's diary, I knew I needed to read the whole thing in some quiet, private place where no one would find me. I went to my secret room.

My secret room was on the fourth floor of the administration building. Getting there involved going through the auditorium, through the halls, into the second floor with its offices and executive dining room.

The executive dining room was only used on weekends now, especially Sundays. The superintendent, the doctors, and others could come there with their families for Sunday meals. The meals were served on tablecloths using real china and good silver. They had waitresses and all.

I always found it strange to think that people who spent their lives trying to help outcasts be more accepted went themselves to nice places set aside for them to dine.

Of course, not everyone saw themselves as helping outcasts. Some just saw what they did as a job. Some didn't give a hoot about us. But others did. They really did.

Anyway, I slipped through that section of the second floor and glanced toward the glass-fronted doors on the small room off to the side of the employee dining room. That was where the steward and his family ate on Sundays. No one was in there now. Then I slipped up the stairs. I couldn't use the elevator. You never knew when it might open on some floor and someone would be there right outside the door. Then you'd be caught for sure.

So I slipped up the stairs to the third and then the fourth floor.

The fourth floor was a kind of throwaway. It had unused apartments where doctors and other higher-level employees used to live. They were one-bedroom or two-bedroom apartments with the most interesting bathrooms. The bathrooms were long narrow rooms with the throne at one end, the tub along one side, and sinks, towel racks, and the like along the opposite long wall. There was a tiled path right down the middle.

The bathrooms were completely tiled with real glass tiles, little bitty ones it must have taken some person hours to lay. The tiles weren't the kind that come in slabs and were just made to look little bitty.

Anyway, this floor wasn't used anymore. All the apartments were empty. My secret room was actually one of those bathrooms in the farthest apartment, clear back at the back.

I didn't have to worry about anyone finding me. No one came to the fourth floor. In fact, the time would come when they took the whole floor off. That happened when they took the large cupolas off too. I hated that.

I always just pulled down the top lid on the toilet, the one that completely covered up the opening, and sat there.

Someone had marked the place they wanted me to read. It had a little slip of paper in it.

"Marcia Weinhart was murdered last month. Only now can I bring myself to write about it," one entry in Adrienne Powell's diary said. It was dated in June of 1934. "She was a friend," Adrienne Powell wrote. "Only a few of us were allowed to see her, even at the funeral home when she'd been taken care of. They said when they found her she was lying there on the altar. They said she had stab wounds all over her body. When I saw her, her face was so disfigured they wouldn't open the casket for the general public."

There was a pause in the diary, and then it took up again:

*As Father Walt completed the funeral mass and said the words which welcomed her into heaven, I had to wonder what people were thinking. The church was full. They all came to judge her and condemn her. Thank God the liturgy doesn't do that, though the people do.*

*Father Coonie had already been sent away. No local priest would bury her. No priest from anyplace around. Father Walt came out of retirement. We all loved him. His thick white hair and soft blue eyes deceived you. They made him look like an aging puppy, but he was too honest and God-fearing to be that. "No one can judge," he said in his homily that day. "God doesn't trade in gossip. God knows our hearts and souls, and only God. Those who came here today to judge should be ashamed."*

And then Adrienne Powell went on with her own thoughts:

*Father Walt knew Marcia Weinhart well. He knew she was too good a Catholic not to be incensed at what her parish priest was doing. If she had known, she would have called the bishop. Father Walt knew that, and I knew it too.*

*Then Father Walt said something which almost knocked me off my seat. He looked out at a church full of judging people, and he said, "Your self-righteous judgment might be because she was a woman."*

*I didn't hear much else from there.*

*When I thought about it later, it occurred to me Father Walt was telling the truth. He was saying that while a male priest might get off for what he did, Marcia Weinhart would be judged and sent to hell by the church and many of the people in it. She would be judged by gossips and hate mongers, not because there was any proof she was a part of all of this, but because the church judges women harshly. Priests can do no wrong. The diocese will help Father Mitch squirrel out of what he's done. He's plainly guilty. He was caught! But there is no proof against Marcia at all. I know she didn't do it! But she was murdered and humiliated. She will be buried in the public cemetery in disgrace. And Father Mitch will get a pass.*

*Churches are so hypocritical! [the diary almost shouted]. Never again will I set foot in this place!*

As I read the pages over for a second time, I could visualize Adrienne Powell burning with anger . . . and helplessness. "People are saying Marcia knew about Father Mitch. I don't believe it," Adrienne wrote. "She was too good a person. If she could have been, she would have been a priest herself. She loved the altar and stayed close to it. She considered it Holy. She's been assigning the altar boys for years. When Father Mitch asked her to assign just one server for the 6:30 morning mass, she did it. She always did what the priests told her to do."

*It is getting nasty [Adrienne Powell wrote later]. I walked out of the bereavement dinner. Noreen McQuain and several others were sitting in the kitchen saying terrible things about Marcia. They were saying Pam Hamlin told them Marcia was involved with Father Mitch. Father Mitch was bisexual, they said. He liked both men and women. I don't believe it. Marcia Weinhart was the finest person I have ever known. She went to mass each day. She loved the children's mass where the schoolchildren go. She took Communion every day and went to confession every week. There is no way she could be guilty of what they say she's guilty of.*

*She raised two children almost by herself. Her husband left her without a cent. Her father's practice, which had been so huge one time, was destroyed by the epidemic. She still lived in his great big old house, but it was falling down around her. The only thing she had left was her good reputation.*

*Gossip is a terrible thing. You can't defend yourself against it, and especially if you've been murdered.*

*So I walked out of the bereavement dinner.*

*Now they are talking about me too. They say I knew what Marcia was involved in. I visited with Sonny Weinhart the other day when he was here closing up his mother's house. I told him how much I loved Marcia. I told him there was no way she could do what people said she was doing.*

*Afterward I wondered if I should have done it. He told me he'd kill Coonie if Coonie were still here, and from the way he said it, he seemed to mean it.*

*I don't understand the diocese. How could they just*

*shift Father Mitch somewhere else? If I were the diocesan bigwigs, I would go to the police. I would encourage those parishioners he and all his priests are supposed to be taking care of to prefer charges. Things would be so much better if they were out in the open. There is no way to defend against gossip and unreal secrets.*

The rest of that year's diary was devoted to defending Marcia Weinhart. The entries never got back to "Warm today. Rain expected." Instead, they reflected the pain of a woman who had no real way to defend her good friend.

And then the diary ended. There were heavy scribblings that tore the paper, and the rest of the pages were just blank.

I never knew for sure, but I always guessed Adrienne Powell never wrote in a diary again. It was almost a given that she was the one who sent the diary to me. According to Nancy Jane (and as I later learned for myself), Adrienne was in her sixties now.

I always suspected she had wanted to try to get justice done in some way or another, maybe by going to the police or trying to get the newspaper to write something, but she didn't have the courage. The diocese was too rich and powerful, and she was used to bowing to their power.

*Maybe Nancy Jane told her friend Adrienne Powell what I was trying to do*, I thought back then, *and Adrienne Powell decided to send her anger off to me in hopes I could do something with it now. Maybe doing that was better than just throwing the book against the wall.*

There's only one person I ever really wanted to tell about where Father Coonie ended up and that's Adrienne Powell, but I never told her.

# 50

At the Little Store and in the Visiting Room

WEDNESDAY, FEBRUARY 3, 1954

have Adrienne Powell's diary," I told Nancy Jane on the
phone. "I need to have you pick it up and take it back to her."

"I'll be out this evening," she replied.

"I visited Adrienne this afternoon," Nancy Jane told me when
she came. "She's the one who sent you the diary. She doesn't
want to see you." We were in one of the empty visiting rooms.

"You'd told her I was involved in all of this?"

"I didn't mean to say your name, but . . ." Her voice trailed
off. "I told her you had heard conflicting things about Marcia
Weinhart.

"Adrienne's my friend, Roy. She is still torn up about what
happened twenty years ago. She still cries about it and talks
about injustice. She hasn't been to church since all this happened, and she hasn't spoken to Noreen McQuain or Pam Hamlin in almost twenty years."

"I can understand that," I told Nancy Jane.

"She bottled it up inside herself," Nancy Jane said. "It was a big thing for her to send the diary. She told me, 'I thought it might act like an eyewitness.' "

"She knows everyone involved," I said. "She knows Larry and George Carson, and, of course, Rosalyn is her daughter."

"She doesn't know Kurt Harrison. He's a newcomer."

I almost laughed. Small towns are a wonder. You don't really belong in them unless you are at least second or third generation, maybe more. No one who comes in is ever a real citizen of a small town. I said as much to Nancy Jane, whose heritage went way, way back.

"Yeah, we have a way of leaving people out but using them as well," she said. "That's what makes us vulnerable. People thought Father Coonie was the most wonderful person in the world. He would do anything for you if you asked him to. We thought we were using him, and all the time he was using us . . . especially Marcia Weinhart."

# 51

⊱—⊱—◇—⊰—⊰

# On the Ward

That night, Harry came to see me on the ward. "I have a word from Larry," he said.

"Larry's coming out of it?"

"Things are tough for him right now. I can't tell how tough, but he wants you to know there was a horrible spitting fight between Kurt Harrison and Rosalyn Pope."

"Harrison accused *you* of spitting on him."

"I suppose Rosalyn gave him the idea. Something happened between Rosalyn and Harrison. Larry don't know for sure. But Harrison grounded Rosalyn, and Rosalyn spit on him and tried to tear his hair out. She hates Kurt Harrison."

"I don't see how that helps," I said, but still it seemed I should follow up.

Later that night I went to the record room. There in Rosalyn's file was an offense report that Harrison had written up in late December. "R. Pope grounded for fighting with another patient," Harrison had written. "Very belligerent. Suggest a workup."

He evidently got what he wanted, because Dr. Jane had written an order for more medication, a lot more medication, the kind of medication that would put you out of it for a while.

We all hated that kind of medication. It took our selves away. Sometimes I think the doctors did it out of self-defense. It was the only real way they had of protecting themselves and other people.

# 52

⊳–◄◆►–○–◄◆►–◄

# Out on the Grounds

**THURSDAY, FEBRUARY 4, 1954**

he next day, I was the one to receive a phone call. Nancy Jane must have known or worked with whichever attendant answered the phone, because they called me to the phone to talk to her. She wanted to meet out on the grounds.

We met near the front gate, not far from the cyprus trees.

Originally, the old institution had a fence around it and an arched entrance with lockable swinging gates. The top of the arch peaked. There was a large metal eagle perched on the peak. The eagle was long gone by the 1950s. The fence had been taken down and the arch removed. All that remained was the winding road up to the main building, but still people talked about the way the entrance used to look.

"Roy, this is Mrs. Powell," Nancy Jane told me when we met. "She changed her mind. She wants to talk to you." Then Nancy Jane walked quite a ways away.

Adrienne Powell looked like a worn, wrung-out dishrag. She was limp, pale, stooped, and weak. "I want to talk to you about Sonny Weinhart," Adrienne Powell said as we both sat down on a bench out near the entrance. It seemed like such a strange place to meet. It was so public. Maybe Nancy Jane counted on the fact that people sitting on the benches were just part of the landscape, ignored by those in cars. People driving up the drive-way hardly looked left or right. After all, it was just those crazy people out there on the benches, people you didn't want to admit existed.

"Sonny Weinhart is Marcia Weinhart's son?" I said just to make sure we were all on the same page. "There are two sons."

"There are two sons, Sonny and Carl," Adrienne Powell said. "They were bitterly angry when their mother was killed, and in a way, I understand. I've never gotten over Marcia's death myself. She was so unfairly treated. So many people said she was a part of the whole thing. She wasn't!

"Sonny and Carl thought Father Mitch killed her. They thought their mother was going to turn him in. I kept trying to tell them their mother didn't know anything about what Father Mitch was doing, at least until near the very end. Sonny and his brother didn't believe me, and the Catholic hierarchy didn't really care.

"Later, Sonny said even if their mother didn't know, as long as Father Mitch thought she did, he would have killed her."

"Did the two sons talk to the police?" I asked her.

"They talked to the police, and the police said they had in-terviewed Father Mitch. There was no way Father Mitch could have committed the crime. He was doing something else at the time. I don't know if the police ever said what."

"Why didn't the two sons just go to Father Mitch?" That's what I would have done if I had been in their situation. I might have gone to him and beat the hell out of him, but whatever I did, I would have gone to him directly.

"He had been spirited away by then."

"Spirited away?"

"They came down in the middle of the night. I swear to God this is true. They came down in a great big black Buick with a young priest driving it. He grabbed up Father Mitch and a suitcase full of clothes and took him to the seminary. It happened that very night.

"I never knew if the bishop even knew about it. I always thought he didn't. I liked the bishop and thought he was a holy man. I couldn't visualize him being a part of all of this."

She was always the good Catholic even though she didn't go to church.

"They thought Father Coonie was at risk," I said.

"Why did they protect Father Mitch?" Adrienne Powell said, tears brimming in her dark blue eyes. "Why hadn't they dealt with that raping SOB a long time ago?"

"They probably do a lot more of that than you would ever know," I said. "Every denomination probably does it, covers up, I mean. Maybe every other kind of institution too."

"There's no justice in this world," Adrienne Powell said.

"Only the justice you help bring yourself."

"Sonny Weinhart came to see me a week or so ago," Adrienne Powell said. "He told me someone told him Father Mitch was back.

"Father Mitch was in cahoots with Kurt Harrison. That's what this person said. But the Weinharts couldn't find Father Mitch. They didn't know where he was."

"Why did they tell you all this?"

"I was a friend of their mother's. We kept in touch a lot over the years. They always appreciated the way I defended Marcia."

"There's more than that," I said. "They wouldn't have told you just for that."

"I had told them I knew someone who was a volunteer in the

195

institution. She was friends with someone else who knew what was going on. They thought I could help them."

"You ratted on me," I said with a little smile.

She laughed. "I didn't know you," she said. "Roy, there's something you've got to understand. Marcia Weinhart didn't do a thing. She was innocent. She wasn't involved in this at all, except someone killed her."

"Do you know who?"

"No. I never did. I never had a clue."

"Rosalyn Pope is your daughter," I said.

"Not that I have much contact with her anymore. I'm closer to Sonny than to Rosalyn."

"They were once involved."

"I always hoped it would work out, especially after Marcia died," she said. "The children of two best friends: It would have almost been like a fairy tale."

"I don't believe in fairy tales," I said.

"Rosalyn didn't either. She ditched Sonny and ran off with Barney Pope. They got married, and then what goes around comes around. Barney ditched her. She went off the deep end, and ended up in this place. I've always been ashamed of that."

"I know," I said. "My being here would make my people ashamed too, if they could know."

"Oh," she said, inhaling sharply. "I didn't mean to . . ."

"You don't need to worry, Mrs. Powell," I said. "I have thick skin. Besides, you have been helpful. You really have."

I motioned to Nancy Jane to come back over and get the poor cowed lady who was so ashamed because her daughter was in the same place I was.

# 53

## From Inside the Institution

### THURSDAY, FEBRUARY 4, 1954

When all hell breaks loose, all hell breaks loose. Thursday evening I saw the first pictures. They were nude pictures of women patients taken with some sort of Polaroid camera. Someone was trying to sell them. I got the impression he was collecting a set of the pictures to ship outside the institution.

Talk about a sticky wicket! Anything involving sex and a place like a state hospital is grist for the media mill, and that was true, even back in 1954. Even with friends in high places, pictures like this could blow things wide open. The world was just barely beginning to be centered on the mass media back then. Even Randall Jessee was a threat. He's the guy who hosted the first Kansas City local newscast on WDAF-TV in the late 1940s. He was still working for them in 1954. He may have seemed harmless enough, but over the years we've learned no newscaster is harmless.

Anyway, a patient on the ward showed me some pictures, and I convinced him to give them to me. He had expected money.

For a little while, I was in a panic. The little man was scheduled to go to the central office again the next day. He was already in hot water for everything that happened. And he was important to me. Without him, there was no guarantee this place would be as humane as it was right then. He believed institutions were only as good as the people who had power in them.

One time I complained to him about how hypocritical churches are. He just looked at me and said, "Roy, institutions are just vessels. They get filled with good or bad according to the people in them."

"Some institutions are plain evil," I told him hotly. One thing I liked about him was that you could disagree with him.

"Those institutions were made by evil people," he said earnestly, as if there was something he really wanted me to learn. "I can show you good churches, Roy. I can show you people who have done great things through some kind of connection to the church. Just take a look at Albert Schweitzer."

Schweitzer had long ago bailed out on the historical Jesus and gone to Africa to help hurting people. You might ask how I know that, but I'm a reader. I read all kinds of things. One time, the little man looked at something I was reading, smiled, and told me, "Roy, you're sure not as dumb as you look." He knew that. He had seen my record. He is the one who had written in it: "Above genius level."

But he was down-and-out right now. In other times, he might find out about these pictures and deal with them quietly, but he couldn't do that now. I had to.

I went to Kurt Harrison. "Kurt, my friend, we've got a problem," I told him, showing him the pictures. He just laughed in my face. "Why should I care?" he said. "Why should it matter to me if this whole place goes to hell?"

"Because I know who beat you up," I said. "I could arrange another beating. I could get word to them that you know more than you have told them." I couldn't really, of course, or actually, maybe I could, but I wouldn't. That wasn't Roy Rogers' way, but Kurt didn't know that.

That seemed to take the sap out of him. He just wilted. "What can I do about a thing like this?" he asked.

"I need to know who's taking the pictures," I said, "and I need to know tonight."

"I can't do that."

"That makes me sad," I said with a little smile.

"I'll do what I can," he said.

Later that night he came to me and said, "It's Mary on . . . ," and then he named the ward. "Her brother smuggled in the camera. She's supposed to take the pictures and then slip them out to him."

"Get me the camera," I said.

"I don't think she'll give it to me."

"You have your ways," I said. "Get me the camera and all the pictures. I don't care what you tell her, but I want all the pictures."

The camera was a Polaroid 95. It was one of those early instant cameras that used roll film. It would be a stalwart in the small-time pornography industry.

Don't let anyone tell you pornography is a new thing. It's not.

"You got all the pictures?" I asked when he came back to me.

"I got all the pictures and all the rolls of film, and the camera itself. Mary had just started. She had decided that maybe she could sell a few of the pictures to the men around here. She had given them to . . . ," he named a name, "and being the brilliant person that he is, the first one he solicits is none other than Roy Rogers.

"I promised her there wouldn't be any consequences to what she tried to do."

"You tell her if she tries it again, there'll be strange things showing up in her record."

"That's what I'll tell her."

"Tell her tonight," I said. "I mean it."

He seemed to understand.

"By the way, Kurt," I said. "Why did they beat you up in the first place?"

"You may be able to get me to do a lot of things," he said, "but I'll never tell you that. They'd kill me."

And of course, he'd told me what I needed to know.

I didn't put it off. I went that night and put a time bomb in Mary's record. It was a simple document made to look like a longtime part of the official record. A few weeks from now, I'd find a way to clue somebody in, and when they found it, they'd think they simply missed it on admission. They'd send Mary to a more secure place.

There was nothing else to do. If she had done the picture thing one time, she would do it again after all this had died down.

That night, I crushed the Polaroid camera to smithereens, as they say, and then put the pieces in the outside trash receptacle. There was no need to have that item lying around. I also burned the pictures.

And by the way, I never did tell the little man that his Albert Schweitzer example didn't apply to the point he wanted to make at all.

# 54

➤─┤─◆➤─❖➤─◆─┤─◄

# The Artist's Room

## FRIDAY, FEBRUARY 5, 1954

That morning I accosted Rosalyn Pope on her way to work. We had ducked into the paint-smelling artist's room right near the laundry. Brandon hadn't come in yet.

Brandon was a terrific artist who did pencil drawings and oil paintings. They had given him a little room to work in.

"You got ticked off at Kurt Harrison. You called Sonny Weinhart and told him Kurt Harrison had been showing Father Coonie around here," I told Rosalyn Pope.

"What if I did?" she said.

"What was the argument about?" I asked. "Why did you spit on Harrison and try to tear his hair out?"

"Roy, you've been reading in the records again. That can get you into trouble."

I felt a little hitch in my stomach. "I don't think you'd rat on me," I said. "There is a kind of ethics to living in a place like this. Inmates don't rat on one another, even to get even. They do other things, among themselves, but they don't rat on one another." I didn't really know how true that was, but I did know she couldn't rat on me without revealing her part in all of this.

She just shrugged.

"My guess is that Sonny and his brother beat up Kurt Harrison. They were trying to get him to tell them where to find Father Coonie."

"There's a kind of a delicious irony about it," she said. "Kurt didn't know what had happened to Father Mitch. There was no way he could tell them. The more he told them that he didn't know, the more they beat him." She was smiling.

"Where was Father Coonie the night Marcia Weinhart was killed?" I asked out of the blue. "Your mother said the police told Sonny Weinhart that Coonie had an alibi."

"When they went to find him, he was in bed with a young man. They had been there all night long."

"Oh, God," I said.

"It just gets worse and worse, doesn't it? Don't let anybody tell you there was one redeeming feature about Father Mitchell Coonie."

"You still didn't tell me what the argument with Harrison was all about."

"Father Coonie wanted me to arrange a meeting between him and Sonny Weinhart. He sent Harrison to ask me. I told Harrison, 'No way,' and Harrison went off. He was gonna get a bundle if I had agreed."

"Why didn't Coonie just go see Sonny Weinhart?"

"Harrison said Coonie wanted to set up a meeting in a safe place. He wanted to have Sonny come to the seminary where Coonie had taught. He must have known what he was trying to do was dangerous. He was looking for safe ground."

"But you wouldn't do it."

"You're damn well right I wouldn't. I wouldn't do anything for Father Mitchell Coonie or for Sonny Weinhart."

"Harrison saved the spitting charge for someone else," I said.

"That amused me," Rosalyn Pope said with a smile. "Here I was, the one who spit on Kurt Harrison, and he didn't even write it down. He saved it, and he used it when he wanted to get at you through Harry."

As I walked back from the artist's room, I thought about how I'd gotten myself between a rock and a hard place. I thought I knew who killed Father Hogan now. It was probably the Weinhart brothers. When they beat Kurt Harrison, he couldn't tell them where Father Coonie was, so he gave up Father Hogan instead. And when they went to visit Father Hogan, he couldn't tell them about Coonie either, so they finally killed him.

If they couldn't get Coonie, at least they could get his lover. But how did Harrison know about the relationship between Coonie and Hogan in the first place? The two men had been pretty secretive about it.

And even if I was right, what was there to do about it? How could I reveal the murderers without involving the hospital?

I needed to protect the hospital. It truly was *not* a place where terrible things happened, though everyone seemed to want to think it was. I couldn't let them jump to their conclusions.

Besides, all this was speculation. I didn't even know who killed Father Coonie. Nor did I know who killed Marcia Weinhart either. How could I get anywhere without knowing all of that?

So, the story wasn't over yet, and the outcome was even more uncertain.

. . .

It was a little later that day when I learned the central office had given the little man an ultimatum: Settle things down within the next month or resign; but that wasn't a great big thing. I knew they were going to do that. It was a part of the charade. As I told you before, the little man had powerful people on his side.

There was another bigger thing. The people at the central office told the little man they received a call from the reigning Catholic bishop.

The bishop viewed the hospital charge as dangerous and was not going to replace Father Hogan. There would be no mass said in the state hospital until "the place was made safe and clean again," as the bishop put it.

Hypocritical SOB! His whole institution was the source of the problem from the beginning, and now here he was passing judgment. And it like to killed the little man. The little man was a Catholic, one of those who didn't attend church much, but still he thought the bishop had the power of heaven and of hell. The bishop may as well have told the little man he was going to go to hell, and even more than that, the bishop didn't tell him face-to-face. Instead, the bishop called the central office in Jeff City.

The first thing the little man did when he returned, I heard, was call the local school superintendent to see if they could rent a school bus on Sunday mornings. "We have a group of patients we need to take to the Catholic church on Sunday mornings," he told the man. By the end of the day, they had a regular Sunday trip to mass all set up.

"Why didn't you just send them to the Protestant worship?" I asked the little man later. "After all, there's Protestant worship every Sunday morning in the auditorium."

"Protestant worship is not the same for a Catholic," he said.

"And besides, they've already missed mass for several Sundays. Mass is important for a Catholic."

"Maybe all churches are a piece of crap," I told the little man.

"Roy, you said it yourself. There's good and bad in everything. There's good and bad in all kinds of religious institutions. Protestant ministers can rape people too."

I just shut up.

>─┤─◆>─○─<◆─┤─<

# 55

# The Little Store and Then on the Ward

### FRIDAY, FEBRUARY 5, 1954

That afternoon, I called Nancy Jane. She was probably sick and tired of hearing from me, except she knew how important all this was.

"Ask Adrienne Powell who called the diocese," I told her. "I could visualize the call being routed to some committee on the priesthood or something. What caused them to come down and spirit Father Coonie out of Sunrise?"

"Adrienne doesn't know who called the diocese," Nancy Jane said later in the visiting room on the ward. "All she knows is that someone called and threatened to kill Father Coonie. Whoever took the call at the diocese believed the threat, and came down immediately."

"And of course, they didn't call the police and tell them," I said.

"No. Adrienne thinks he was afraid to do that because it would blow Father Coonie's cover. Those aren't her words; they're mine. She put it more discreetly. Of course, she didn't know the police already knew of Father Mitch's proclivities."

"Everyone's been a little too discreet in all of this," I told her bitterly. "If the church allowed their priests to marry, things would be different."

"What does that have to do with all of this?"

"Well, they could allow their homosexual priests to come out and be who they are too. Those folks could have healthy relationships rather than resorting to rape."

"Roy!" Nancy Jane said. She was flabbergasted, and that's when I knew the little man had won me over. I wouldn't beat up any more homosexuals. I was taking his side now.

# 56

## On the Wards

A s if things weren't complicated enough, Harry decided he missed Bullet. Harry sneaked down to Dr. Jane's in the late afternoon, stole Bullet, and hid him back on the ward under his bed.

Bullet stayed there quietly for a long time, but, not long after lights-out, Bullet became impatient and started barking.

He didn't bark just a little. He barked a lot. Harry tried to get him out from under the bed and out of the ward, but Bullet wiggled loose and went running through the ward and up the stairs.

Before anyone could do anything about it, Bullet ran across a little hall and into the women's wing, with Harry following.

Then, of course, all hell broke loose. The women started screaming, and Harry was caught on the ward without any reference to Bullet, who had skedaddled through one ward and up the stairs into another ward.

Just to make things better, Bullet jumped up in the middle of some sleeping woman's bed and when she screamed he peed on her.

By the time they got a hand on Bullet, he had nipped an attendant and run downstairs and out an outside door back toward Dr. Jane's house.

The only thing that saved Harry that time was that Dr. Jane had had Bullet vaccinated, so Bullet didn't have to be killed and examined and the attendant didn't have to take those horrible shots.

But Harry was in hot water again.

When I talked to the little man about it, all he could do was laugh. "I needed something to make me quit thinking about my troubles," he said, laughing. "But only Harry knows how to do it in a way that stirs things up big-time."

So Harry got off light again.

# 57

## In the Auditorium

SATURDAY, FEBRUARY 6, 1954

ometimes the strangest things stir up ideas. Saturday night, they had a movie instead of a dance. The little man must have gotten stubborn in his old age, because it was another Roy Rogers movie, *In Old Caliente*. When I talked to the little man about it later, he told me, "Having Roy Rogers movies is certainly the least of my problems right now. I just decided to do whatever I wanted to do." I take it somebody just gets a list of available movies a few days or maybe even weeks before and they mark the one they want for a particular week. The little man had been the one to do that for the last while.

*In Old Caliente* is from the late 1930s. Roy and his sidekick Gabby Hayes are accused of a robbery (they are almost always accused of doing something wrong). Finally, they set a trap for the real robbers. Roy and Gabby set up another situation where the robbers will attack them, and when the robbers do that, they trap them. The most ingenious thing about the trap is that Roy and Gabby take the gold the thieves will try to steal and have it molded into a two-hundred-pound ball. When the good guys are bushwhacked, the first thing the good guys do is release the mules hauling the gold wagon, so the thieves will be stuck with no way to get the gold away quickly or to divide it up, once they have it.

Roy Rogers was a clever fellow. That's the thing I learned that night. I needed to be clever to make headway, and I, like the Roy on the screen, didn't have a lot of time to make headway.

# 58

## On the Grounds

urt Harrison told me you're the one who told him Father
Coonie and Father Hogan were connected," I told Rosalyn
Pope. It was a whole different kind of trap than the Roy
Rogers on the screen had laid, but still it was a trap using inge-
nuity and all that.

"I thought you told me inmates didn't rat on one another?"

"Harrison's not an inmate," I said. "He's a guard."

"In any case, he ratted."

It made me feel good to know I had lied to her and she didn't
even know it. Harrison had refused to tell me anything.

"You helped cause a murder. Did you know that?" I asked
Rosalyn Pope.

"No, I didn't."

"Sonny and Carl Weinhart beat up Kurt Harrison, and when
Harrison couldn't tell them where Coonie was, they went to Father Hogan. They ended up killing him. At least, I think that's
how it happened."

"You'll play hell proving it," she said. "One thing about being Roy Rogers," she went on. "Your Roy Rogers is so clever he can't tell anybody anything he figures out. After all, it's only Roy Rogers and his sidekick Harry Tonto who know where Father Coonie is."

"Tonto is the Lone Ranger's sidekick."

"It's all the same to me," Rosalyn Pope said.

"I think you killed Father Coonie," I told her quietly. "Either that or you had somebody with you, maybe Sonny Weinhart, and he killed him."

She didn't reply.

"You know Coonie is dead," I went on. "You know I found the body in the record room. The only way to know that is to be the one who killed him or the one who witnessed his murder.

"That's how you knew about Coonie and Hogan. Coonie told you before you killed him."

"So much speculation," Rosalyn Pope said. "Besides, what does it matter? You can't prove it, and you can't even reveal that Father Mitch is dead.

"You know, Roy, I don't understand all this. Why get all worked up because a horse's ass like Father Mitch was killed? And why worry about Father Hogan either? Neither of these people is worth a tinker's dam."

"There's a right way and a wrong way," I said quietly. "Killing is killing, no matter who is killed or what he's done. Besides, I think Father Hogan was probably basically a good man."

"There won't be no justice," Rosalyn Pope said, "unless it's done right here on earth. Whoever killed Father Mitch killed somebody who deserved to die. Whoever killed Father Mitch done the world a favor. They did justice."

"And whoever finds them will do justice too," I said.

# 59

# Around the Wards

## MONDAY, FEBRUARY 8, 1954

I had to wait until Monday to talk to Kurt Harrison. He was working again, three to eleven just like always. But he was more subdued now. He was being careful not to do anything that might bring attention to him or help him get in trouble.

"Rosalyn Pope told me she's the one who told you Father Coonie and Father Hogan were lovers," I told Kurt Harrison that night. "When the Weinhart brothers beat you, they beat that relationship out of you and then went and killed Father Hogan."

"Damn her," Harrison said of Rosalyn Pope.

"Now all you have to do is tell the police what happened. Then they can arrest the Weinhart brothers on suspicion of murder."

"Yeah, and I'm about as likely to do that as you are to jump off the administration building at midnight," Harrison said. "I'll take my chances by just keeping quiet."

"If the police knew you were showing Father Coonie around, they might suspect you of killing him and hiding him."

And Harrison said just what I thought he'd say: "All that

involves the hospital. I'd bet my bottom dollar you won't force anything that makes all this involve the hospital and your sacred little man."

Kurt Harrison was right.

Almost immediately, I went back to Rosalyn Pope. "Kurt Harrison is threatening to tell the police that you're the one who called Sonny Weinhart and told him about Coonie and Hogan," I told her. As long as I was lying, I might as well continue lying and see how things unraveled. I felt pretty good about what I was doing, except I knew the real Roy Rogers would probably hate it.

Rosalyn Pope puffed up like an adder, but she didn't answer.

That night, I slept well. After all, I thought I'd done a good day's work, and now I had to wait to see what happened.

# 60

# On the Ward and in the Auditorium

## TUESDAY, FEBRUARY 9, 1954

found a good one, Roy," the little man told me. He was just quickly walking through the ward, hurrying the way he always did.

"A good one?"

"A good Roy Rogers movie."

"I thought we weren't gonna have any more for a while. We just had one Saturday."

"I changed my mind," he said with a little smile. He didn't bother to say that things had changed. Everything was going sour for him, or so it appeared, so he was just gonna do as he pleased. We could be having Roy Rogers movies twice a week. "The movie's *My Pal Trigger*," the little man told me.

"Oh." That almost took my breath away. "*My Pal Trigger* is only six or eight years old. It's the best Roy Rogers movie so far."

"I had to pull some strings to get it," he said with a smile.

• • •

Later I talked to Harry. "We've got a movie to go to."

"I don't want to go to a movie," Harry said. "I want to play with Bullet."

"This one's about animals, Harry. It's one of the best movies about animals ever made."

"Does it have dogs in it?"

"No, but it's got horses."

"That's almost as good," Harry said.

I thought about telling Harry the movie was a sad one, but I didn't. I was afraid if I did, he wouldn't come. I knew he'd like the movie, but . . .

That night Harry brought Bullet to the movie.

"We can't keep Bullet here," I said. We were sitting near the back row on the men's side. Harry had hidden the dog under his folding chair. The folding chairs were kind of odd. I haven't seen any like them for a long, long time. They were hitched together in long lines, made to be set in rows in a place like this auditorium. That formed a kind of tunnel under each row of chairs.

"I wanted Bullet to see this too," Harry said. "Bullet loves animals. He's an animal himself."

And no matter what I said to Harry, he wouldn't sneak Bullet out.


If you haven't seen *My Pal Trigger,* you should. It is the most powerful Roy Rogers movie ever made. It's the story of how Trigger came to be.

In the story, Roy has a mare named Lady. Gabby Hayes, who is called Gabby Kendrick in the movie, owns a ranch that raises Palomino horses. He has this wonderful horse named Golden Sovereign.

Roy wants to breed Lady to Sovereign, but Gabby won't let

him because Gabby won't get the foal. So the horses run away. They cohabit or whatever you want to call it, and then they are attacked by a wild black stallion. The people who are looking for them include the bad guy—in this movie a true real bad guy. He owns the next ranch. He also owns a casino.

He and two of his ranch hands find the two stallions fighting with Lady looking on, trying to help. The bad guy tries to shoot the wild stallion. He shoots Sovereign instead. The horse dies.

The scene with Gabby kneeling over his dead horse is the most powerful scene Gabby Hayes ever played. But that comes later.

Before that, when Gabby and his daughter ride up, the bad guy is gone and Roy is the one beside the horse. It looks like Roy killed Sovereign.

And by that place in the movie, Bullet has slipped away from Harry. Bullet is making his way through the chair tunnels, down to the end of the row, and then up the aisle into another tunnel up the way. In the process, he moves to the other side of the auditorium. The women sat on one side of the auditorium and the men on the other. I could just visualize Bullet nipping some woman patient on the ankle and causing her to jump up screaming. That would probably happen about the time Roy was being tried for the murder of the horse or escaping on Lady and making his way across several states.

Of course, there's a woman in the story—Dale Evans. She is Gabby Kendrick's daughter. She wants to like Roy, but she's convinced he killed her dad's best horse.

As I watch Bullet pop in and out of the chair tunnels, making his way up toward the front, the rest of the audience is watching Lady have her colt. Because the colt came sooner than they all expected, Roy says he is quick on the trigger. Roy names him Trigger.

Before that, Roy had been almost impoverished, even having to sell his valuable silver saddle to get a bag of oats for Lady.

It's a sad story, but it gets even sadder later.

As the young Trigger is being trapped in some brush and is about to be attacked by a mountain lion, I see Bullet sitting on some lady's lap. She's just petting him like wild and watching the movie for all she's worth.

The strange thing is that, in all this, Bullet never makes a sound. He moves back and forth and lets himself be petted by a lot of ladies, sometimes propping himself up on some woman's shoulder and licking her cheek, but he never makes a sound.

By the time Trigger is being attacked by a mountain lion and Lady is running to protect him, Bullet is in front of the auditorium. And by the time Roy is having to shoot Lady to put her out of her misery because she has been mortally hurt in the fight with the cougar, Bullet is in front of the screen, his shadow looming on the picture. No one seems to care. You can hear people crying, but you don't hear a word about Bullet.

Before this part happened, Roy tells Trigger something. Roy tells him he has a lot to learn about life. Life isn't all easy. Life is interesting, Roy said. "Sometimes it's fun, and sometimes it's tough." And then later he adds, "You gotta take the breaks the way they come."

The thing I like about the movie *My Pal Trigger* is that Roy Rogers proves his own words wrong. There are all kinds of terrible things that happen, including the deaths of two wonderful horses, but the story doesn't end there.

Roy goes back to give the colt Trigger to Gabby Kendrick. Gabby doesn't have sense enough to take Trigger. In his grief for Golden Sovereign, Gabby has almost gambled away his whole ranch playing roulette in the bad guy's casino. Gabby's ranch was in his family for four generations. Gabby ends up betting the ranch on a single race, his horse against the bad guy's. And the bad guy has worked it around so that the horse he owns is Trigger.

If Roy wins the race, the bad guy will give him Trigger. But Gabby will lose the ranch. When the race is close, the bad guy's henchmen try to box in Gabby's horse, ridden by his daughter, and Roy helps her break loose from the box. After that, because they tried to help, Roy and Trigger are behind. They end up losing to Gabby's horse by a nose, though it's clear they tried their best.

So it looks like Roy loses Trigger, which he doesn't, but I'm not going to tell you about that. That's one of the best and most believable plot parts of any in a Roy Rogers movie.

Need I say it? By now, Bullet has dodged through all the tunnels, this time on the men's side, and is sitting on Harry's lap. I promise you, this is the God's truth. That little dog did all that without making a sound and almost without being noticed, except when his shadow loomed large upon the screen. Maybe Bullet did like movies about animals.

As we were leaving, the little man called me aside. "You got away with it," he said.

"With what?"

"With having Bullet here and not causing chaos. I was watching him and wondering what would happen."

"Roy Rogers is right. Life has its ups and downs," I told the little man. "But sometimes we can act to change that."

"Sometimes we can," he said.

"I didn't like that movie very much," Harry said as we were leaving. He was still crying.

"Why not?"

"I don't like to see animals being hurt or killed. Roy Rogers killed one of them himself."

"He didn't have any choice, Harry," I said.

Harry was crying now. "I know that," he said, "but I still didn't like it."


That night, as I thought about *My Pal Trigger,* I wondered what the movie must have meant to Roy Rogers and Dale Evans. They had a lot of hard things in their lives. Roy's first wife died, and Roy and Dale lost several children.

I wondered if Roy and Dale really believed what he told Trigger: Life has a lot of hard breaks in it, but you gotta take the breaks the way they come.

They must have believed it. How could they have been the good people they were without believing it?

A lot of people see Roy Rogers movies as a bunch of fluff. I see them as lessons in life, good lessons, and I thank God for Roy and Dale.

# 61

# On the Ward and in the Horse Barn

## TUESDAY, FEBRUARY 9, 1954

We took Bullet back to Dr. Jane's and then came to the ward. When we got to the ward, Harry was still crying. "It was just a movie, Harry," I said. "He didn't really kill his horse."

"I don't like seeing horses killed."

"But it all worked out."

"I knew someone who killed animals," Harry said. "My father killed my animals, and George Carson's father killed his."

"George Carson's father killed his animals?" I said.

"He killed the neighbor's animals too. George told me that one time. He said he grew up with his father killing animals. He would kill them and bury them in his backyard or other places."

"That's terrible," I said. I didn't tell Harry pathological killers often started out by killing animals.

"George's mother knew about it. She didn't seem to care. George said she seemed to like it too."

"Maybe she was just afraid," I said.

"It all makes me sad," Harry replied.

"Let's go see Pat and Mike," I said. "After everyone's asleep, let's go to the barns and visit Pat and Mike."

And that's what we did. We left by the usual way, down through the auditorium, by the record room, through the employee cafeteria, and out the bakery. Then we made our way over to the barns.

"I'm glad you're OK," Harry told the horses.

"Some animals are well cared for," I told Harry.

"I like the little man," Harry said, "but I like the steward more. At least most of the time. He loves cows and horses. I love cows and horses too."

"He is a nice man."

"He kills cats. I don't like that about him."

"Well . . ."

"But I guess we can't be perfect," Harry said. His grief was clearing up a little. "We need to make a better world for animals," he said.

In later years when I thought about this conversation, I wondered if Harry had followed Roy Rogers. I wondered if Harry had known how much Roy loved Trigger. I even wondered what Harry would have thought if he had known Roy had Trigger mounted and displayed when Trigger died. I've not been able to go see Trigger, but I understand Trigger is still on display.

That always seemed odd to me—having a horse like that mounted and displayed—but Roy was a good man. I guess that was the only thing he could think to do with the horse he loved.

# 62

⊳━┥◆⟩━┥◯━┥◆┝━┥◁

# In Front of the Willow Tree

## THURSDAY, FEBRUARY 11, 1954

Nothing happened for a while. Then on Thursday, Nancy Jane called me. "We're in trouble, Roy. I need to see you."

When she got there, she was in a panic. "Sonny and Carl Weinhart came to visit Adrienne Powell. They told her she needed to quit talking to me and you. They told her what had happened was in the past and it needed to be left in the past."

"They probably talked to Kurt Harrison too."

"I understand he is looking for another job."

"Maybe either Kurt Harrison or Adrienne Powell will go to the police," I said.

"Adrienne did. I could hardly believe it," Nancy Jane said. "It's as if she got some courage somehow. I don't know what changed her, but she went to the police and told them Marcia Weinhart was innocent of what everybody said. Then she told them several other things.

"At first they seemed to think she was just off her rocker, but then when she talked about Kurt Harrison's beating and about Rosalyn Pope, they stopped to listen."

"What happened then?"

"They are going back over the whole thing again. They called Sonny and Carl in and visited with them. They are planning to come back out here again, to talk to Rosalyn Pope."

I felt my stomach tighten. Rosalyn could tell them about Father Coonie. She could only do that by admitting she was the one who killed him, but if they were closing in on her, she might give me over too. Right now, of course, they didn't even know Coonie had died, but if they stirred enough . . .

"When I talked to Adrienne, she told me she had prayed about going to the police. She told me the answer she got back was that she herself is a part of the problem. She needed to have the courage to stand up and do something.

"She even looks different, Roy. She looks like she has some dignity now."

"That's good," I said. "The little man always says, 'If you can't avoid real trouble, you might as well wade into it head-on. It comes to get you either way.' "

When I got back to the ward, I found a note under my pillow. The pillow had been placed in such a way that I knew to look. We patients in the hospital weren't any different from others who were somehow restricted or confined. We figured out our ways to communicate.

The note was from Rosalyn Pope asking me to meet her.

She ducked out of lunch, and we met in the artist's room beside the laundry. "I've decided to tell you the truth," she said.

"The police are going to interview you soon," I told her.

"Yeah. They're coming this afternoon. I thought I needed to get things straight with you before I talked with them."

"You killed Father Coonie."

"No, not really. You probably won't believe this, but it's the truth. I had a note to meet him. When I did, he told me he decided it didn't work to go through Kurt Harrison. He himself needed to visit with me.

"He was pathetic, Roy, all bloated and red. He didn't seem to make much sense sometimes. Sometimes he cried, and sometimes he cussed. He said he was a sinner. He was going to roast in hell. God had told him personally he had to go to everybody and ask forgiveness. He had gone to a lot of people. They had cussed him or ignored him or hit him. One even pummeled him with his fists. Some broke down crying, but he had tried to go to them. These weren't just men in Sunrise. These were people all over the place. He'd served in a lot of parishes.

"The hardest ones were the ones like us in this place. He finally connected with Kurt Harrison through Father Hogan, and Harrison got him access here.

"I even asked him about Marcia Weinhart. He said Marcia Weinhart was just a pawn. She didn't know why he wanted just one altar boy at six thirty. She just let him pick the altar boys, and then she scheduled them. She did whatever he said to do. She'd been doing that for priests all her adult life. She didn't know she was scheduling abuse.

"He had caused her, in her innocence, to die, he said. Those were his very words, 'caused her, in her innocence.' "

I started to say something.

"Let me finish," Rosalyn Pope said sharply. "Now he had to talk to Carl and Sonny. He needed to ask them for their forgiveness."

"He told you about Father Hogan too."

"He said he met Kurt Harrison through Father Hogan, and I could tell there was something there. I kept pressing him until he told me about his love for Father Hogan. I like to puked."

"And then you killed him."

"He had a fit. He swelled up like a toad and died. I didn't lay a hand on him."

"He was all beat up, Rosalyn. He even had his nose broken."

"I helped kick him into hell, that's all. I didn't touch him until he was dead there on the floor, and then I kicked him into hell. I stomped on his face, just for good measure.

"He caused all this, Roy. Later I loved Sonny Weinhart, and Sonny was still so tied up in what had happened to his mother that he didn't give a damn about me. He was filled with hate. He still is. He just used me and then threw me away. All he could talk about was the injustice in the world and if only he could get his hands on Father Mitch.

"They kept Father Mitch locked up in the seminary, Roy. Oh, he went places sometimes, but he always went back to that protected place, that place where a slob like Sonny wouldn't have had a chance of sneaking in.

"Sonny's hatred never got any less, Roy. Sonny hated Father Mitch as much ten years later as he had hated him the day it happened."

"So what do you want from me?"

"I didn't kill Father Mitch. Not that I wouldn't have liked to, but he died first. Besides, I wouldn't have killed him because I would have gotten caught. I wasn't smart enough to get away with it.

"Now, if they know about him, they're gonna think I did kill him. You cover my ass by keeping Father Mitch hid right wherever he might be, and I'll cover yours.

"You might think I'm not worth a bucket of warm spit, but we're in this all together now. We need to look out for each other."

And I agreed.

# 63

## On the Ward

T he police came to see me before they went to talk to Rosalyn. This time it was the chief himself, a big man with a huge beer gut. He had some peon with him.

"Son, you're involved in all of this," he said. "Everywhere I turn, your name crops up. We thought it was that little horseradish named Harry for a while, but then we figured out it was you."

"I don't know anything about it," I replied.

"What happened to the priest?" he asked.

"I don't even know the priest," I said.

"We think you may have killed him. Or you know who killed him. He came out here one night and he never came back. That's what we think."

Maybe they had talked to Father Hogan before he died. Or maybe Kurt Harrison had finally cracked.

"I didn't come from Sunrise," I said simply.

"We know that. We've checked that out. You didn't come from anyplace that . . . ," and he used a word I wouldn't reprint here, "You didn't come from anyplace that 'person' served."

I just waited.

"Harry's next," the chief cop said. "If you won't break, maybe your friend Harry will."

Later, I learned that when they talked to Harry and tried to grill him, he started talking about Bullet. "Bullet's a wonderful dog," he told them. "He can sniff out quails and he even barks at cows."

Later that night, I received a note from Rosalyn. "Have talked to Sonny and to Kurt Harrison," the note said. "They have both clammed up and won't say anything."

# 64

## On the Ward

That night I didn't sleep much. As Roy Rogers I faced a dilemma. There had been murders. There was no doubt about it. Even if I accepted Rosalyn's story about Father Coonie's death, which, by the way, I did, Marcia Weinhart and Father Hogan had been murdered. Real murder. No simply swelling up like a toad and dying. Father Coonie's heart may still have been beating when Rosalyn Pope stomped on him, but she didn't think so. I was sure of that.

You may wonder why I accepted Rosalyn's basic story. I couldn't visualize her bringing Sonny into the institution. In fact, I couldn't visualize her doing anything to help Sonny kill Father Coonie. And she wasn't a killer herself. At least not in as physical a way as Father Coonie had seemed to die. She might have shot him if she could have gotten away with it—used an impersonal way to kill him, so to speak. But she wouldn't strangle him or beat on him . . . unless she thought he was already dead.

We don't think about it often, but there are personal and impersonal ways to kill people. Marcia Weinhart was stabbed at least one hundred times. Whoever did that was mad as hell. He, and I did think it was a he, wanted to kill her in an up close and personal kind of way.

I knew a sniper once, from Vietnam. He mistakenly killed a Vietnamese mother holding a small baby who was a long way away. He said it didn't bother him that much until a few weeks later when he saw another Vietnamese woman up close. She had been killed the same way. Now his dreams were haunted with the mother he had killed. She was always there holding her baby, and she always had the face of that other woman.

So, as Roy Rogers, I had a real problem. I could help all these people clam up for a while. In fact, there was no other choice. But in the long run, I had to help see justice done. Without justice, Roy failed. Roy always brought justice.

One of the things that amazed me about *In Old Caliente* was that when the bad guys bushwhacked the gold shipment, you could see some of the men in the movie—both bad and good— being shot off their horses.

Everyone talks about Roy Rogers as if there is no killing in the Roy Rogers movies. There is killing. In that movie, the Patron was murdered. But Roy Rogers never kills anybody. Roy Rogers always finds a way to bring justice to the world without killing.

Talk about a more perfect world! Roy Rogers showed the way. Confront evil, but don't kill.

It always pleased me that the Roy Rogers up there on the screen was so much like me.

# 65

# On the Grounds

**FRIDAY, FEBRUARY 12, 1954**

Because I didn't much like George Carson, I had stayed away from him. Now, as things unraveled, I needed to confront him.

"It's all beginning to fall apart," I told him as we walked out on the grounds. "The police are looking into it again." I was going to try to reason with him, push him into telling me what he knew. As it turned out, I didn't need to do that.

"I know we need to stick together," he said. He seemed different, more subdued.

"You should talk with Rosalyn Pope. She'll tell you we're all in this together now," I said.

"She already has. She told me we should all keep quiet."

"And we need to share the things we know with one another."

He just grunted.

I paused, trying to think of what to say.

"Rosalyn told me you killed Father Mitch," he said quietly.

"If they find him, it will all come out," I said.

"She said if things came out, we'd all be involved. She said we needed to keep everything quiet, but if the police finally did get on top of it, you killed Father Mitch and hid his body somewhere."

I just let George think whatever he wanted to think.

"I want to thank you, Roy," he said quietly. "You did me a big favor when you killed him. I said too much to that bitch Alice once, but this is different. You have done a good thing for me." So, now I knew why our relationship had changed.

"You told me Marcia Weinhart was in cahoots with Father Coonie," I said.

He didn't answer.

"How did you know that?"

"She's the one who scheduled me to be an altar boy. I was just a kid. I thought the church was holy. I thought everyone involved with it did sacred things."

"And Father Coonie raped you."

"Again and again over several months. I didn't know any better. I felt terrible and dirty, but I didn't think I could tell on Father Mitch. He was the priest. He had been chosen by God to be there."

"When did you tell your parents?"

"I didn't. My father caught us. He suspected something. He followed me to mass one day. That's what broke the whole thing open and caused Father Mitch to go away. My old man found me and Father Mitch in the robing room."

"Why didn't he just beat the hell out of Father Coonie?"

"He was too busy beating the hell out of me." The words fell like the dull clank of one of Hoss' hammers on his anvil. In my own mind, I could see the priest cowering in the corner while this huge man beat his son, landing terrible, hard blows on the boy's arched back and arm-covered head.

"He dragged me out of there and went on beating me. He

beat me for several days. I kept crying and saying I didn't mean to do it, and he just beat me more and more.

"Finally, he told me, 'This will teach you. You have to be a tough son of a bitch. You have to hate fags and weaklings.' I've tried to do that ever since."

But I knew now, the role of tough guy didn't fit George Carson. Whatever else he was, he wasn't violent in the way this father had wanted him to be.

"By the time my old man decided to quit beating me and to start beating Father Mitch instead, Marcia Weinhart had been killed and Father Mitch was gone. They had come down and taken Father Mitch away."

"Who killed Marcia Weinhart?" I asked.

George Carson didn't answer.

"And what destroyed your sister?" I went on. "She's in the insane asylum cemetery now. That's where she chose to be buried. What does she have to do with all of this?"

"I don't know," George Carson said. He was crying.

"Your father is the one who killed Marcia Weinhart," I said simply. "He had killed animals before.

"I don't know exactly why he killed Marcia. Maybe he couldn't get to Coonie, so he got to Marcia instead."

"No, that's not how it was," George Carson said. "I told you Marcia Weinhart was killed before Father Coonie left. If my dad had wanted to kill somebody, he could have killed Father Mitch, not Marcia Weinhart. Besides, my old man would never hit or hurt a woman. Never. He worshiped the ground my mother walked on. He thought women were sacred objects. It was a part of his code. His code was, beat the hell out of other men and honor women to your dying day. Don't pay any attention to your women. See your women as kind of glorified servants, but honor them."

"So who killed Marcia Weinhart?"

"My mother did."

I must have taken a deep breath.

"She pleaded with my father not to beat me. Over and over again, she kept on pleading. Then she became fixated with Marcia Weinhart. They had been friends.

"She kept saying, 'How could Marcia set those children up for Father Mitchell? How could Marcia set *my* George up for Father Mitchell?'

"She came to think Marcia was more guilty than Father Mitch was." And then George Carson added: "That's not so strange when you think about it. My father thought my rape was my own fault. He thought Father Mitch had turned me into a fag or, worse yet, Father Mitch had been seduced by his own son, who was already perverted. A homosexual is the worst thing you could be in my father's eyes." I felt sad for him. He was sexually confused himself. How could you help but be?

"My mother thought Marcia Weinhart had turned Father Mitch into a rapist, and my father thought I had caused Father Mitch to rape me because I was perverted too. That's how my family thought."

"So your mother killed Marcia Weinhart."

"She drugged Marcia in our own home, and when Marcia passed out, she stabbed her with a kitchen knife. No one except little Melissa was home. She watched.

"When my father came, he helped clean up. That night he took the body and dumped it on the altar."

"Where is your mother now?" I asked. I was worn-out. I'd never heard such a pathetic story.

"She's dead now, Roy. Have you ever heard of people who have willed themselves to die? One time Father Hogan told me about a little old woman who was seriously hurt in an accident.

After she went to the hospital, she had to go to the nursing home for a while. She had always promised herself she would never allow anyone to put her in a nursing home. She didn't understand this was just for a while. To her a nursing home was a nursing home.

"She pulled her bed as close to the wall as she could get away with, turned her face to the wall, and died. It took six weeks or so, Father Hogan said, but she did die."

"And your mother did the same."

"After Melissa died and was buried out here, not in the family plot, my mother did the exact same thing. She pulled her bed up against the wall, climbed in, turned her face to the wall, and finally died herself. She hardly said another word. It's hard to believe people can will themselves to die, but they can. I watched it."

"There must have been a terrible fight about Melissa's being buried here," I said.

"Father Hogan took my side in all of that. Melissa had written a note about what Melissa wanted. That's one time when I stood up for what I believed. My father even sided with me. He told me, 'It's her last wish, her last will and testament so to speak. You don't go against someone's last wish.'

"I told you he was a man with a strange code."

"All I know to say is that I'm sorry," I told George Carson.

"Don't be sorry, Roy," he replied. "You didn't have anything to do with all of this. Besides, you killed Father Mitch, and that's good enough for me."

So we were buddies now. Murder makes strange bedfellows, so to speak. Now it was people like George and Rosalyn and Hoss and Harry and me against the world. Now we needed to find a way to get all this worked out to bring justice without involving the good people and things around us. That would be a hard thing, even for someone like Roy Rogers.

# 66

## On the Ward

FRIDAY, FEBRUARY 12, 1954

So now, I thought I knew the whole story. Three deaths, and I thought I knew who caused them all. Rosalyn Pope had watched Father Coonie die, probably of natural causes. The Weinhart brothers had most likely killed Father Hogan after having beaten Kurt Harrison. And George Carson's mother—oddly enough he never said her name—killed Marcia Weinhart.

But what good did all that do me? Those were my thoughts on Friday night. I couldn't prove any of it, and even if I could, I wouldn't be able to protect the good guys in all this.

One thing I had done, I had visited with Harry. "You can't tell anyone about this," I told Harry.

"I know. When they try to get me to tell things, I just talk about Bullet."

"That's a good thing to do," I told Harry.

"We need a witness," Harry said, almost offhandedly.

"What's that?" I asked.

"We need a witness," Harry said. "I know how these things work. Philip Marlowe would tell you that we need a witness."

# 67

# The Little Store

SATURDAY, FEBRUARY 13, 1954

I called Nancy Jane that afternoon. She all but hung up on me.

"I can't be a part of this anymore," she said. "All we've done is cause more trouble. Adrienne Powell is in the midst of a mental breakdown."

"I had hoped she was some kind of witness," I said.

"She's been to the police. She's told them everything she knows. I'm just sure she has, Roy. She doesn't have anything more to say."

"The police have interviewed the Weinhart brothers again," I said.

"And that didn't lead anywhere. The police have even come to see me. They told me they thought I had been giving you information. They said I had been the link between Sunrise and 'that guy out there who thinks he's Roy Rogers.'"

"I lied to them, of course," she said. "I told them I didn't know what they were talking about. But I can't be involved in this again. I have to bow out."

I tried to answer, but she cut me off.

"I want to be polite here, Roy," she told me. "I'm going to hang up the phone, but I don't want to just slam it down."

"Thanks for all you've done," I said. "I'll call you later." And she hung up . . . gently.

From there, I went to find Kurt Harrison. He didn't usually work on Saturdays, but often he was around a lot. That in itself should have been suspicious, but I don't guess it was.

"He's quit. Gone. Kaput," an attendant named Maud said. "He came in yesterday and cleaned out his locker. He said this was too crazy a place for him to work."

"Did he say where he was going?"

"To work, you mean? He didn't say. He just said he'd find something else. He was a friend of . . . ," and she gave me the name of the man who ran the hospital pig farm.

The hospital hog farm was down the way off the country road that led toward the cemetery. The man who ran the place was known to be a nice man. He was just an old hog farmer who did what he had been doing all his life.

Hogs are one of those things that changed over the years. I knew a farmer back in the fifties who said, "You can pay the mortgage with hogs. Cattle are up and down, but those sows, they have a lot of babies."

So most farmers, at least in Missouri, raised hogs, and so did the hospital farm. That was almost half a century before corporate hog farms.

"He just told me he was leaving," the old man said when I went to ask him about it. The old man was out doing his final chores in the evening. He didn't seem to resent me asking about Kurt Harrison. "He didn't say where he was going or why. But he was in an awful hurry."

I wondered if Harrison felt at risk. He might have.

"If he gets in touch with you . . ."

"You know I can't do that, Roy. I wouldn't rat out a friend any more than you would. What's sauce for the goose is sauce for the gander."

So that was that. There was no contacting Kurt Harrison. I had to use whatever resources were at hand.

# Out on the Grounds

### SUNDAY, FEBRUARY 14, 1954

Sunday was Valentine's Day, but I never paid too much attention to that. Saint Valentine was some kind of a saint in the church—the saint of love, I think. I don't believe in love. I believe in friendship and mutual caring and even sex. I know sex is real because I've seen the beautiful and the terrible things it can do. But I don't believe in love. I ignore things like Saint Valentine's Day and just go on about my business, which is what I did on this Valentine's Day.

"You were a friend of Father Hogan," I told George. We were walking on the grounds again. It was the most private place we could find.

"He helped me get Melissa buried out here at the hospital. I want to be buried out here too. The place will probably be gone by then. I don't know if I'll have anyone to fight for me."

"We don't control things when we're dead," I said.

"That's when we need others to fight for us."

"Anyway, Father Hogan tried to help you when it came to Melissa."

"He helped me in all kinds of ways. He counseled me when I was depressed. He probably calmed me down and kept me out of lockup at least fifty times.

"Everyone talks about the priest who was here before. The old man who did the woodworking. They forget Father Hogan has been here almost ten years."

He was right. I had forgotten how long Father Hogan had been here. "Did he come on to you?" I asked.

"Father Hogan?" George pulled back from me. "Of course not! He was just a friend. He never even touched me, never even shook my hand."

"That's strange."

"I don't care what he was, Roy. He wasn't like Father Coonie. I told him that one time. I said, 'I don't care what you are,' and he said, 'You're one of the few, George. You're one of the few.'"

"He kept a diary," George Carson said out of the blue. "He read me some of the poems he had written in it."

"A diary or just a book of poetry?" I was floored.

"Both, really. He said he had a 'secure' hiding place here at the hospital because there were people in his house he wouldn't want to pick it up and read the personal things in it."

He didn't want Father Coonie to read it, I thought. "What all did he share with you?" I asked.

"Only poetry and stuff. It didn't matter much to me except he wrote it. He said he learned to keep a journal in a seminary class. He said it had stuff in it which he didn't share with anybody."

"I wonder where he hid his diary?" I asked.

"He didn't say."

# 69

# On the Prowl

SUNDAY, FEBRUARY 14, 1954

That night I made my way to Father Hogan's office. For some reason, it seemed dangerous to me, so I waited till way late. It was out-of-the-way, on the third floor of the administration building, in one of those old apartments, so isolated, no one would see my flashlight. Like all the offices, it had several rooms, but they were being used differently than most of the converted apartment rooms in the other offices.

The smallest room, a little bedroom, was his office. It had a desk, with books on it, including what looked like his ecclesiastical office book, a little book with the prayers he was supposed to say. That book was thumbed and worn.

The front room, which was the largest, had couches and chairs. It looked like he used it for counseling and the like.

And the back bedroom was just that, a bedroom. He had a single bed in it, a dresser, a mirror, and things like that. He sometimes slept there. He was the chaplain, after all. There were times he needed to be at the hospital late at night. Maybe someone was dying or maybe there had been some kind of sudden illness and there was family to sit with or console.

Anyway, there was a lot to search, and as it turned out, the search was fruitless. There were clothes in the dresser and toiletries in the long, narrow bathroom. The bathroom was set up just like the bathrooms in the other offices.

I looked under mattresses, in the little closet in the bedroom. I even stood on a chair and shined a flashlight back into the deep top shelf of the closet. I looked in the toilet tank. People often hide things there.

I looked in the little kitchenette, especially the freezer. I thought he probably wouldn't hide anything there. He knew enough old people and how they often liked to hide things in their freezers. Besides, the cold might cause his diary to deteriorate.

I took up cushions and pushed on pillows to try to find the diary, but I didn't find it.

Maybe this time he had taken it home. Maybe the Weinhart brothers had found it when they killed him. If so, they had probably burned it in their backyard burning barrel.

It was too late to do it tonight, but as I left the office, I thought of one more place to look. It was the only other likely place I knew of. If there was some third place, I'd probably never find it.

# 70

## In the Chapel

MONDAY, FEBRUARY 15, 1954

I had to wait until the next night to make my way across the back lot, through the outside door, through the tunnel, and to the chapel. That's the only other place I could think of where he might have hidden the diary.

First I searched the confessional. Somehow that seemed appropriate. After all, it was a confessional document of a sort.

I looked under the cushions and even got down on my knees to look under the chair where the priest sat and then under each of the fastened-down kneeling benches in the penitents' compartments. The diary wasn't in any of those places.

Then I got down on my hands and knees and looked under each of the handmade pews. If it had been me, I might have taped the book under a pew. Few people would think to look there. For one thing, you had to get down on your knees.

I looked through some carelessly stacked books. The best way to hide something is with other things just like it. I looked in the book holders in the pews.

I took the robing room apart. I went through each of the

vestments—the white under vestments and the embroidered outer vestments. The outer vestments were somewhat worn, as if they had come secondhand from some other church. But the diary wasn't in the robing room.

I was just about to give up, about to close the door to the chapel, when it occurred to me that there was one more place. The altar itself. In the tabernacle there with Jesus!

It took a little while for me to get the tabernacle open. It was a simple lock. Almost too simple. I was careful not to jimmy it.

When I got in there, I found a covered chalice with bread hosts in it. They must have been the prayed-over ones. They must have been Jesus.

On the floor of the tabernacle, there was a feltlike cloth. When I lifted that cloth, I found the diary. It was hidden there with Jesus. It made a little cloth-covered platform on which the chalice stood. Even if someone was saying mass, he might not have found it, but no one was saying mass. The bishop had cut the hospital off, not allowing them to have a priest.

I took the diary, replaced the felt, took the chalice, as carefully as I could—it was something holy—and put it back in place. I even said a little prayer as I closed the door and worked the lock back shut. I didn't exactly believe all the things these people believed, but that didn't keep their beliefs from being holy.

I tucked the diary in my shirt, unbuttoning the shirtfront and letting the little book rest at my waistline where my belt was. That was the only place I had to hide it as I made my way up to my secret room.

Once I was in my secret room, I could turn a light on. The bathroom had a window in it, but there were shutters on the window and they were always closed. They were old shutters, well made and sealed tight with old coats of paint. The light didn't much get through.

I had everything I needed, a toilet, and running water in the sink if I should need a drink of water, but I didn't think I'd need a drink.

I read the diary all the way through. It was much more personal than Adrienne Powell's diary had been. But it didn't have salacious things in it. It just had little notes:

> *I am hiding this from Father Mitch. He's the one who taught me to keep a diary. He taught us all. Even when he was in the parish, he taught classes to the laity on how to keep a diary as a spiritual exercise, and now here I am, hiding my diary from the man I love.*
>
> *Father Mitch receives threatening letters from Sonny Weinhart. He has for years. The only thing protecting him is that he is at the seminary. He's almost cloistered, though it's not that kind of place. I pray each time he leaves there to come see me.*

That note was written several years ago. It was in a tight, cramped hand, as if he wanted to make a lot of words fit in a small space. There were others similar to it, almost up to the present time.

> *Father Mitch is becoming more and more irrational. I talked to the little man about it, not telling him who I was asking about. The little man said there was a lot medical science didn't yet understand about old age and dementia. People became remorseful "sometimes for good reasons and sometimes not." They also became irrational, he said. Some became bitter and angry, not easy*

*to handle. Only medication seemed to settle such people down, at least some of them, but the downside to that was that sometimes it took so much medication, they almost lost who they were. The little man offered to work with whatever friend I was inquiring about, but I told him that just would not be possible.*

*I talked to the little man about how epilepsy might or might not add to the problem. "Epileptics often have severe depression," the little man said. "That would add for sure."*

Early in the diary, Father Hogan expressed his feelings for Mitchell Coonie. Father Hogan also talked about how he had worked with Father Mitch—counseled him—to stop doing the terrible things he had been doing. For a long time, Father Hogan expressed his idea that Father Mitch might not be able to change. "Father Mitch himself was an abused child," the diary said. "I told him that's no excuse. We still make choices. He didn't have to rape people just because of his own situation. There is a difference between rape and love."

"I wonder if mental illness is hereditary or learned?" Father Hogan asked in one part of the diary. "My counseling with Father Mitch leads me to believe I could help some troubled people. The Pope would die if he could know who I really am and how Father Mitch has taught me about God!"

Early on, Father Hogan expressed his own disgust at what Father Mitch had done before he knew him. Father Hogan also expressed his anger at the church and at the diocese. "I can't reveal this to anyone," he said. "I think the church has fault in all of this. I am most pained about Marcia Weinhart. Whoever killed her had the whole thing wrong. In all this, she is the most innocent of all."

Later, Father Hogan said something quite revealing: "There is precious little I can do about what has gone before. In one way, God has given us a slight reprieve. He has allowed me to help get Melissa Endicott buried out here, the way she wanted. He has helped me counsel her brother who doesn't even know I know what he is facing. I didn't want to come here because of Mitch's ties to Sunrise, but the bishop sent me. Now I think I see God's working, even in this."

As I read those words, I was struck by the part that said: "God has given us a slight reprieve."

I took the "us" to be himself and Father Coonie. Father Hogan was trying to atone for not just his own sins but the sins of Father Coonie too.

As I read the diary, I came to see Father Hogan as a strange kind of person who was simply trying to work out his own salvation. I had heard him say mass, and I had heard him preach a lot. After all, I went to mass with the Catholics, mostly because that's where the little man attended church sometimes. But still, I didn't really know Father Hogan.

Now I thought I knew him.

There was one more note, one of the last: "I've been threatened too. The Weinharts have been stalking me."

I was pushing it, and I felt odd. It was getting late, but that same night I made my way to the mail room. I had to hurry. It was just a couple of hours before dawn and patient wake-up, but so be it. This had to be done.

249

There were all kinds of things in the mail room, sharp knives for opening mail, stamps to be used by hospital personnel and sold to patients, envelopes, and all the rest.

I cut out one particular page of the diary, the one with the note about the Weinharts stalking Father Hogan, as well as a few other pages, found a plain envelope, put the pages in it, sealed it, put stamps on the envelope, and then addressed it to Red at *The Sunrise Sentinel.*

That wasn't all I did. I found the outgoing mailbag. It was about two-thirds full of outgoing mail from the last part of the previous day. I shook about half those envelopes out. Put my envelope in way down in the middle, put the other envelopes back in, and scooted off to the ward as silently and quietly as possible.

When they did the morning wake-up, I was in bed, supposedly asleep.

That morning, maybe because my part in all of this was over, my demons overwhelmed me. They swarmed around me and tied me down for almost two weeks.

It started happening early in the day. At first I was OK. I went down to the little store and phoned Nancy Jane. Then I set out on my errands. As I walked, I could feel my demons start to surround me. They followed me as I made my way from the willow tree to the old barn where the horses were stalled.

I was barely in charge enough to check to see if the grave was still protected. I wanted to make sure Father Coonie was still ensconced there, not trying to work his way to the top. Now that things were mostly taken care of, I didn't want Father Coonie coming to the surface ruining it all.

I must have looked terrible. "You're gonna have a hard night tonight," Harry told me when he saw me later in the morning.

"Is there anything I can do?" He meant it. He was trying to be helpful, but there wasn't anything he could do.

"I'm fine," I said. We both knew I was lying.

I went to the commissary and talked to my friend there. He had stashed more overalls where I could find them. "You can get them when you need them," he said, glancing at the hiding place. They were just in a box up on a high shelf where no one ever looked. Years later, I often wondered what those people did, the people who were rummaging through the old empty hospital to see what was there. They must have found a lot of shelves with hidden or forgotten items. Or maybe they just tore the old place down without even looking.

By afternoon, I was almost immobile. The little man had been to see me. He increased my medicine. "Focus on the right thing," he told me, but I was so tied up in knots, I hardly heard him.

I didn't eat that night or probably for several days more. The demons just kept coming at me in waves. They wanted to attack me, take me down, and do terrible things to me.

They weren't dreams. I can't emphasize that enough. No one who compares what happened to me to a dream can understand. What I faced was real.

Before the whole thing was over, I was pissing on myself and doing other things I won't mention. I wanted it to be different, but I couldn't make it different. I was totally in their control.

Along with the demons came the waves of blackness. Some would call it depression, I suppose, but it was more than that. It was despair.

I don't believe in the devil, in Satan and that kind of crap, but if there was a devil and if there was a hell, I was in it. The flames of both mania and depression licked around me and eroded the

251

very nature of my being. It was as if I were being washed away, owned, raped, torn apart by forces beyond anyone's control.

And I lashed out. I fought. I pounded the walls and tried to bend the bed rails. When I was manic, no amount of medicine would calm me down. And when I was depressed, I was so deep in hell, no amount of medicine would pick me up.

"We don't want to use too much," I heard the little man say through the fog one time. "We don't want to put him out completely."

I didn't understand it. Why not put me out? For some reason, he wanted me to keep on fighting. Then it occurred to me, it wasn't fighting he wanted me to do. He had told me, I needed to focus on the right things.

But what were the right things? I saw Father Coonie's body there before me, still lying in the record room, still lukewarm as it was when I found it.

I talked to Father Coonie. "Why did you do what you did?" I asked. And he replied, *It didn't do me any good. It didn't make me happy.*

"That's no answer," I replied. And, as dead as he was, he turned his head so his dull, blank eyes were staring at me and he told me, *You're Roy Rogers. You aren't violent. You do good.*

That's all he said.

And then the blackness overwhelmed me.

But as I was swimming through the blackness, I kept hearing: *You're Roy Rogers. You aren't violent. You do good.*

One time I heard the little man's voice from another time and place: *Never give up on anyone*, he said, *and try not to let them give up on themselves.*

I had to try not to give up on myself.

It was as if the little man was trying to help me hang in there. And it was as if that pervert Father Coonie wanted to teach me something he had never learned, or at least had learned way late in life. After all, rape is an act of violence, not a sex act.

Violence only feeds the demons, the little man had told me. Anger only makes them stronger. Maybe I should use some kind of good to struggle with them. Maybe instead of seeking out the fags and killing them . . . I felt a wave of hatred almost overwhelm me and the demons become stronger. . . .

I don't know how to make this part of what was happening to me real to you. When I start talking about coming up out of the darkness, I know my words won't be as clear as they were in blackness. I'm afraid my words will seem contrived.

I remember once the little man said, "It's OK to be angry, Roy. You've got a lot to be angry about. But finally, you've got to get beyond it."

In a way, I think Roy Rogers would have hated it that I found him. He would have said he was just another man. He was a Christian, and he would have told me about Jesus. I think I need to say that to be fair to Roy. But Jesus didn't work for me. I had seen too much hate and evil in the people who lived for Jesus. If Roy lived for Jesus, then maybe Jesus helped me, but . . .

Still, the depression lifted. I focused on a good man, Roy Rogers, and on his wife, Dale Evans, too. I even asked God to help me do something good, and God seemed to reply, *You have.*

My prayer and God's reply didn't overwhelm the demons, but it calmed them down some. Doing something good seemed like something I could work on. I could place my focus elsewhere, so to speak.

There are religious traditions based on meditation. I've never understood those, but as I came out of all of this, I sort of came to understand. What I thought about mattered. How I responded *in my heart and mind*, even to the terrors in my life, made all the difference.

So gradually, I came back to the life I usually led. I couldn't have done it without the medicine and the help from other people, but I came back different this time. I came back knowing there was another way. The demons would still raise their heads, sometimes terribly, but I could have a different focus, and when that occurred to me again (I did forget it sometimes) I was better. I was not the best, but I was better. I guess that's all anyone can ask.

➤—┤◆╶╼○╾╴◆├—◅

# 71

# The Rest of the Story

T he rest of the story can be told quickly, though it didn't happen quickly. It was several days after I put my letter in the mail before *The Sentinel* had the headline "Suspects Held in Murder of Priest." There was a subheadline that said: "Beating Victim Is a Witness in the Case." The story appeared while I was still out of it. I just saw it later.

According to the story, *The Sentinel* had anonymously received Father Hogan's diary pages in the mail, had verified they were in Father Hogan's handwriting, and had turned them over to the police.

They photographed each page, of course, before turning them over, and printed excerpts.

Like I told you, I had called Nancy Jane the morning things started going sour for me. "I know you don't want to talk to me right now," I said, "but this is important."

"I can't be involved," she said.

"You have to take my word for this," I said. "I'm not going to ask you to do anything you won't be willing to do. Red will be receiving something in the mail. I need to send a message to him."

"What message?" she asked.

"Tell him, I did what he wanted me to do. Now he needs to do two things. First, don't involve the hospital. Get the hospital out of this no matter what."

"And second?" she said.

"Protect Father Hogan. Don't smear Father Hogan in the newspaper. If there's a trial, some of this might come out. But don't smear Father Hogan in *The Sunrise Sentinel*."

"I can tell Red those two things," she said, and then she told me thank you. She must have trusted me again. She thanked me without even knowing exactly what it was I had done.

Later, *The Sentinel* had a headline "Excerpts from the Diary of a Murdered Man." Nothing in the excerpts they printed even hinted at the sexual relationship between the two priests. Of course, the pages I sent them didn't have a hint of that in them either.

Still later, there was an editorial:

*Aside from all the victims themselves, the most aggrieved people in this whole terrible mess have been the people at the mental institution. People have believed terrible things were happening out there. We all know the rumors.*

*We owe the hospital staff and patients an apology. No. We owe them more than that. We owe them our support. The payroll of the institution is at the heart of the economy of this community, and the problems it deals with are problems that communities like ours have helped create.*

*It is time for all the rumors to abate.*

In the end, they couldn't keep Father Hogan out of it entirely, but *The Sunrise Sentinel* didn't smear him, and because they didn't, the story was a whole lot more subdued than it might have been.

Even Roy Rogers isn't perfect. There was one thing in the story that I never did work out. I never learned who had called the diocese and threatened to kill Father Coonie. Given what he did, there were a lot of folks to choose from.

# 72

## My Final Thoughts

I don't expect anyone but family to be reading this. When you do, I will be long gone. There are a few things I might say:

First, it feels good to know that Father Mitchell Coonie spent a lot of years with some horse or other pooping on him. At least I think that's probably what happened. Finally, they closed the hospital, of course. I don't even know if the big barns are still there, but for a long time the barns had horses in them.

In closing the place down, they moved us out, put most of us in nursing homes. Then they turned the old insane asylum into another kind of place, serving mostly mentally handicapped, not mentally ill. And finally, they just tore the buildings down, not all of them, but most of them.

One time not long after they had moved us, the little man came to visit me in the nursing home. I asked him, "What's really gonna happen to all those people?"

"They'll end up on the streets and under bridges," he said. And he was right. A lot of them did end up under bridges or in prisons and jails.

So now you know the rest of the story, except for a little part of it I never told you: I've always liked the story of the song "Happy Trails." I didn't hear the story until sometime later.

The song was written in 1950, the year Roy and Dale's daughter Robin was born. "Happy Trails" has a line in it that says it's how you ride the trail that really counts. Roy and Dale had to live the meaning of that line. Their daughter Robin was born with Down's syndrome and other medical complications. They sought the best medical help possible, but instead of putting her in an institution, they took her home and loved her. Robin died in 1952. Roy and Dale also had two other children, Debbie and Sandy, die in accidents. So Roy Rogers and Dale Evans were special people, people who faced great tragedies with strong Christian faith. They cared for and loved children, their own natural and adopted children and all children.

That was so much different than it was for me.

Do you remember that I told you about the most evil man I ever knew? He went to a very prominent mainline Protestant church each Sunday. He got up every Sunday morning, and on most Sundays he raped his young son before he showered and shaved and went to church.

He was considered a holy man in his church—the one who made it possible for it to be as beautiful as it was. He had paid for the restoration of the sanctuary. He was a rich and venerated man. He was my father.

Remember, I told you once, I'd seen too much hate and evil in Jesus. I saw it through my father. He was flaunting his faith, always saying things like, "Praise Jesus!"

One Sunday morning as my father was raping me again, I decided there had to be a better world somewhere. When I found it, I would live in it.

Years later, I saw my first Roy Rogers movie, and I found my world. Roy and Dale always rode the trail right, no matter what they had to face. The "Happy Trails" song says some trails are happy and some are blue, but "it's the way you ride the trail that counts." Roy and Dale rode the trail well. They always wished you "happy trails." Roy Rogers never really hurt anyone, even the bad guys.

One time, the little man said, "Roy Rogers is a good example for you, but I think you know you're not really Roy Rogers."

The little man was almost always right about things, but he was wrong about that. I am Roy Rogers. Roy Rogers always lived his life right.

I chose to be Roy Rogers before I'd even heard of Roy Rogers. I chose to be Roy Rogers almost as soon as I knew about Roy Rogers. And I will always be Roy Rogers, no matter what.

Happy trails!

# A CONCLUDING NOTE
# FROM JOE BARONE

In the first half of the twentieth century, there were hundreds of mental institutions across this nation. All of them were inhumane to some of their patients and perhaps, at times, to all. And surely there were way too few people who, like the little man, tried to reform the existing mental health system, tried to make mental hospitals more humane. But there were many such people.

I didn't write this book to cover up the abuses of mental hospitals. Books such as Jim Lehrer's *Flying Crow* (about a runaway Missouri mental patient) and historical exhibits such as the display of the contents of suitcases found at the Willard Psychiatric Center in New York's Finger Lakes region clearly remind us of the terrors to be found in such places.

I wrote this book to remind myself again of a forgotten group of abused and hurting people. Those people were my playmates, among my best friends as I was growing up. I look back on them with great respect and love. I want to honor them. I want them to be remembered.

Every character in this book is fictional, but like the real people I grew up with, they each have a history, a reason for being who it is they are. And many of them are good and valuable people, maybe more good and valuable than some of the people on the so-called outside.

Make no mistake about it. The neglect and abuse of the mentally ill continues. In my own state, hardly a month passes without some newspaper article about the neglect of the mentally handicapped or the lack of state funding to meet the needs of the mentally ill.

Not long ago, CBS's *Sixty Minutes* ran a segment on the deaths of several mentally ill people in the prison system where many thousands of mentally ill people are now housed.

Mental hospitals were what they were because society wanted them to be that way. And mental treatment today is what it is because we want it that way.

I've heard it said that it is easy to condemn a group—the Jews or the Negroes or the "illegal aliens" or the Muslims or the gays. But when you get to know one person in that group, maybe when you are a child or when you need help and that person provides it, your view changes.

My view was changed in childhood. I want to honor those I write about. Make whatever criticism you want of the way I portray mental hospitals, but don't forget the people in them. And don't forget the people who, despite the wishes of society, worked, sometimes at great cost, to make those places more humane.

With that said, I hope you enjoyed meeting Roy Rogers, Harry, Bullet, and their friends, and I hope you will look forward to meeting at least some of them again.